"Crider's skill is portraying distinctive characters. . . . Highly recommended."
Booklist

"The characters are especially interesting."
The Daily Oklahoman

"The story moves along at a quick pace."
Rave Reviews

"Sheriff Rhodes is a different, commonsensical, delightful character."
Publishers Weekly

DEATH ON THE MOVE

Bill Crider

IVY BOOKS • NEW YORK

Ivy Books
Published by Ballantine Books
Copyright © 1989 by Bill Crider

Library of Congress Catalog Card Number: 88-28051

ISBN 0-8041-0425-5

This edition published by arrangement with Walker and Company

Manufactured in the United States of America

First Ballantine Books Edition: September 1990

To Pet and Eldred Stutts

Chapter 1

"YOU GOTTA COME to the funeral home right now." Clyde Ballinger's voice on the telephone was urgent. "It's important."

Sheriff Dan Rhodes knew that Ballinger wasn't kidding. Whatever he wanted would have to be important to keep Ballinger away from his usual Saturday-morning rounds, which consisted of visiting every garage sale within a ten-mile radius of Clearview and looking for old paperback books.

"I'll be there as soon as I can," Rhodes said. "What's the problem?"

"I don't want to talk about it on the phone," Ballinger said. He had lowered his voice considerably. "It's something to do with business."

Business? Rhodes thought. Had there been a murder that he didn't know about? Ballinger's business as a funeral director brought him into contact with nearly every dead body in Blacklin County, and he and Rhodes had formed a sort of friendship on the basis of their occasional encounters.

Rhodes hung up and turned to Hack Jensen, the dispatcher, general flunky, and resident wit of the county jail.

"I'm going to run over to the funeral home," Rhodes said.

"Might get there quicker if you'd take the car," Jensen said, without cracking a smile.

Jensen seemed to think that part of his job was to find jokes to make, and when he got together with Lawton, the jailer, Rhodes often found himself thinking he was trapped in some vaudeville routine. Fortunately, Lawton was back in the cellblock and Jensen was having to go it alone today. Rhodes didn't resent their playfulness: for what the county was paying them, they deserved a little fun.

"Good idea," Rhodes said. "I think I'll do that. I'll give you a call back after I talk to Ballinger to see if anything else's come up."

"You tell Clyde I said hello," Jensen said. "But that's all. He's been looking at me too close lately, like he's measurin' me for one of those boxes of his."

Rhodes wasn't sure exactly how old Jensen was, but he was far beyond retirement age. That was why the county got him so cheap. He was willing to work for next to nothing as long as they gave him a place to keep busy. He had to be well over seventy, though he didn't look it, and Rhodes was sure that Ballinger wouldn't be measuring him for any box for a long time.

Rhodes went out to the car. It was a beautiful day for January, almost no clouds, the sky so blue that it seemed to go on forever. The temperature was in the middle sixties, and Rhodes didn't even need a jacket. He knew that a norther could blow in any day and drop forty degrees off the thermometer in a few hours, but he was hoping that wouldn't happen for a long time. It wasn't much of a hope, though. January wasn't a month in which you could count on many sixty-degree days.

He drove on over to the funeral home in the county car. He didn't stop in the front. He knew that if Ballinger wanted to talk to him in private, he would be in the little house behind the main building. The funeral home had once been one of the finest private homes in Clearview, and Ballinger had converted the old servants' quarters to his own hideaway after he bought and renovated the place.

Rhodes tapped on the door and Ballinger let him in. As always, Rhodes was amazed by the room. The walls were lined with shelves of paperback books by obscure authors, and Ballinger had read most of them. His special favorite, however, was Ed McBain, and he never seemed to tire of telling Rhodes about the exploits of the members of the 87th Precinct. In fact, there was a hardcover book on Ballinger's desk. The title was *Tricks*, and McBain was the author. He was the only author Ballinger bought in hardback.

Ballinger looked uncommonly glum, but he cheered up momentarily when Rhodes mentioned the book. "Yeah," he said. "It's pretty good. Better than the last one, that's for sure. It's about Halloween, and people start finding arms and legs and things in trashcans." He paused and looked at Rhodes. "Matter of fact, it reminds me a little of what happened around here not so long ago."

Rhodes didn't want to hear about it. He remembered all too well the episode to which Ballinger was referring, and it wasn't necessarily a pleasant memory.

"I guess you didn't call me to talk about that, though," Rhodes said.

Ballinger looked around the small room as if someone might be hiding behind a book and listening to them. "No," he said. "I didn't call you about that." He walked over and stood behind his desk, looking down at the McBain book.

He seemed almost at a loss for words, a situation which rarely occurred. People often thought of funeral directors as taciturn men, gloomy and professionally suave, but Ballinger wasn't like that at all. He was always cheerful, always ready with a joke, almost a glad-hander. Rhodes had never seen him so quiet.

"Maybe you ought to sit down," Ballinger finally said.

There was an old rocking chair across from the desk, and Rhodes sat in it, moving a copy of a paperback Western titled *Saddle the Storm* to make room for himself. He put the book on the desk beside *Tricks*.

"You want to tell me about it?" Rhodes asked.

3

"Not really," Ballinger said. "But I guess I better."

They sat there in silence. After what must have been at least a minute, Rhodes said, "Well?"

Ballinger sighed. "I got the Storms over there in the other building. You know the Storms?"

"Jack Storm?" Rhodes asked.

"That's him. Him and his wife, Elva. They're sitting over there waiting on us, but I don't know how to face them. Nothing like this has ever happened before."

"Like what?" Talking to Ballinger today was almost as bad as talking to Jensen and Lawson. He could never get a straight story out of them, either.

Ballinger looked around the room again. "Theft," he said.

Rhodes didn't think there was anything new about theft. "Who's the thief?" he said.

"I don't know," Ballinger said, shaking his head. "That's the trouble. The Storms think it's me."

"That's ridiculous," Rhodes said. "What would you steal?"

"Nothing," Ballinger said. "But if I didn't steal it, who did?"

"Steal what?" Rhodes asked.

"You think Tom Skelly would steal?" Ballinger asked. Skelly was Ballinger's partner.

"Slow down a little bit," Rhodes said. "I think I must be losing the thread of the story."

"It's not a story," Ballinger assured him. "It's the truth."

"Okay, it's the truth. But let's find out what the truth is. Something's been stolen, I got that much. But I don't know who stole it or what it is. I'm not even sure who's getting accused of being the thief. At first I thought it was you, but now I think it might be Tom. The guys at the 87th would have you in the back room and be getting out the rubber hoses by now."

"They don't do things like that." Ballinger looked offended. "They do good, honest police work."

"I'm sure they do. But then maybe they manage to get a straight story anyway."

Ballinger stood up, walked over to his bookshelf, and

started idly running his hand over the spines of his collection. "I'm sorry, Sheriff," he said. "It's not that I don't want to tell you about it. I guess I'd make a lousy writer."

"You don't have to write it. Just tell me. Start at the beginning and go right on through to the end."

Ballinger returned to his seat. "I guess it all started when Jane Storm died."

"That's Jack's sister?" Rhodes asked.

"Right. She died yesterday afternoon. The funeral's supposed to be on Sunday."

"Supposed to be?"

"Yeah. The Storms came in to see her this morning, see how she was laid out, see if we did a good job. You know."

Rhodes knew. He nodded.

"Of course we always do a good job. Tom's one of the best in the business. Never too much makeup, always just the right expression on the face. A real artist."

Rhodes didn't say anything. He was sure Tom Skelly did good work, but it wasn't an art that Rhodes wanted to think about. He remembered how his wife had looked, and all the art in the world couldn't have made her look the way she really had, the way he remembered her.

"Anyway, they came in to look at her," Ballinger went on. "They noticed right off."

Now they were getting to it, Rhodes thought. "Noticed what?" he said.

"Noticed that her ring was missing," Ballinger said. His voice was hushed, and he looked down at the desk.

"Her ring?"

"It was the one her mama gave her—gold band, big diamond solitaire in the middle. She never did get married, Jane didn't, so when she was about thirty-five her mama gave her the ring. Figured she wasn't ever going to get one any other way, I guess."

"Storm tell you all this?"

"Right. After he found out it was missing, he did."

"And it was on her when they brought her in?"

"Well, no," Ballinger said. "But they brought it by later. They wanted her to be buried with it on."

5

"Do people do that much?" Rhodes said. "Bury their family in their jewelry?" He had buried his wife in her wedding ring. He remembered that.

"All the time," Ballinger said. "Except for the greedy ones."

"And the ring's not on her now."

"No. And her earrings aren't on her, either."

"Earrings?"

"Gold ones, with diamonds. Came along a few years after the ring," Ballinger said.

"Anything else?" Rhodes wondered.

"Her necklace," Ballinger said. "Pearls."

"Pearls with diamonds?" Rhodes said.

"We don't question their taste," Ballinger said. "We just do what they ask us to do."

"And Tom put the jewelry on her when he dressed her."

"That's what he says. And I believe him. We've been partners for years, and we make a good living out of this place. Why would we want to steal something like that?"

"But somebody stole it," Rhodes said.

"I guess so. It couldn't just disappear."

"And you want me to talk to the Storms." It wasn't a question.

"They're talking about a lawsuit," Ballinger said.

"I guess we better walk on over there, then," Rhodes said.

"Thanks," Ballinger said.

"All part of the job," Rhodes told him.

Jack and Elva Storm were sitting in the Peace and Grace Room, on the back row of the metal folding chairs that sat on the thick gray carpeting. The walls were painted a peaceful bluish gray, and soft music was being piped into the room over several discreetly concealed speakers. Rhodes thought he recognized "Peace in the Valley."

The casket holding the mortal remains of Jane Storm sat on a dais in front of the room. It was supported from underneath, probably by sawhorses, Rhodes thought, but you couldn't tell because whatever was holding it had been concealed by a cloth drapery.

Jack Storm heard them enter the room and stood up, turning to meet them. He was a tall, thin man with very white hair and a red face. He was wearing a dark suit that looked as if it had been bought twenty years before but not worn very often.

He stuck out his hand, and Rhodes shook it. "Heighdy, Sheriff," he said.

"Hello, Jack," Rhodes said. "I understand there's some trouble here."

Storm looked out over to where his wife was sitting. She was short and plump, and she sat with her hands clasped in her lap. She was looking at the floor, or maybe she had her head bowed for prayer. Rhodes wasn't sure which.

"Maybe we could step outside," Storm said. "All this has hit Elva kinda hard."

"Of course," Ballinger said. He ushered them outside the room to stand in the hallway, which was covered with the same thick carpeting.

"You have some property missing?" Rhodes said when they were outside the room. He noticed that he was whispering, which he guessed was only natural, considering the surroundings.

"That's right," Storm said, looking accusingly at Ballinger. He was whispering, too, but his whisper was harsh and throaty. "My sister's ring, her earrings, and her necklace. They was worth a lot of money, too, Sheriff. A lot of money. Sure, we was gonna bury 'em with her, but that was sentiment. If somebody stole 'em,"—he paused and looked at Ballinger again—"well, we'd have to sue. After you put the thief in jail, that is."

"I think I understand how you feel, Jack," Rhodes said. "But I think Clyde, here, is an honest man. Something's wrong, all right, and I'm going to find out what it is. Maybe it's just a mistake."

Storm didn't look even halfway convinced. "What kind of a place is it where there could be a mistake like that?" he said.

"It might be something else," Rhodes said, but he didn't know what. "Don't worry. I'll find out."

"What about my sister?" Storm said.

"Your sister?"

"Yeah, my sister. What about her funeral? You don't think we're gonna let this fella"—he glared at Ballinger—"put her in the ground without her jewelry on, do you?"

Rhodes hadn't thought about it, to tell the truth. "It might be possible to delay the funeral," he said.

"Better not be much of a delay," Storm said.

"We'll do all we can," Rhodes said.

"I hope so," Storm said. "I want this taken care of right now." He turned and went back to join his wife in the Peace and Grace Room.

"Where's Tom?" Rhodes asked when Storm was out of earshot.

"You go on back out to the office," Ballinger said. "I'll get him."

Rhodes walked across the asphalt parking lot and entered the office. While he waited, he thumbed idly through one of Ballinger's books, *River Girl*, an old Gold Medal book by someone named Charles Williams. Rhodes started reading a passage about a man weighing down a dead body with an outboard motor in order to dump him in a lake. Ballinger and Skelly came in, and Rhodes put the book back on the shelf.

"That's a pretty good story," Ballinger said. "I think the guy who tells the story is a deputy sheriff. He gets involved with this woman, and then he—"

"Never mind," Rhodes said. "How are you, Tom?"

Skelly looked more like a funeral director was expected to look. His suit was dark black, and his face was thin and drawn. He looked as if he had never smiled, though he wasn't frowning. His mouth just seemed to turn down naturally at the corners.

"Not too good," he said. "I guess Clyde's told you what happened."

"He told me about the missing jewelry," Rhodes said, "but he didn't tell me how it happened."

8

"I guess he couldn't," Skelly said. He had a deep voice, like the bass singer for a country quartet. "We don't know what happened, exactly."

"Did you ever see the jewelry?" Rhodes asked.

"Sure. I'm the one who put it on her," Skelly said. "I always do those things. It's my job."

"You're sure you remember doing it?"

"Sure I'm sure. I don't forget something like rings and necklaces."

"When was the last time you saw her?"

Ballinger spoke up. "We put her in Peace and Grace around two o'clock. We could look at the register to see what time she started having visitors."

"And she had the jewelry on then?"

"She must've," Skelly said. "But I don't remember checking."

"And I didn't bother to check," Ballinger said. "Tom's never made a mistake about anything like that in his life."

"So between somewhere around two o'clock yesterday afternoon and this morning whenever the Storms came in, the jewelry was stolen," Rhodes said. "Is that about right?"

"That's about right," Ballinger said. "Unless . . ."

"Unless what?" Rhodes said.

"Well, I hate to say something like this, but do you think maybe they took it? The Storms, I mean."

Rhodes thought about the Storms and everything he'd ever heard about them. It didn't amount to much, but he'd certainly never heard anything about them that would lead him to think they would steal jewelry off a dead woman. In fact, he couldn't think of anyone he'd ever heard of who would do a thing like that.

"They do seem pretty anxious to sue us," Skelly said. "Maybe they need money real bad right now. They could sell the jewelry, and get the insurance, too."

"I'll check into it," Rhodes said. "See what I can find out. At least you've got insurance."

"We won't have much of a reputation, though," Ballinger said. "Not if this gets out."

"That's true," Rhodes said. "Let me check up on Jack

9

Storm's finances. Then I'll talk to him, see if I can find out anything.''

"You do that, Sheriff," Ballinger said. "We're counting on you. It's times like this I wish we had the 87th Precinct down here in Texas. I bet Carella and Hawes could get right to the bottom of it.''

"I'll try to do halfway as well as they could," Rhodes assured him, but Ballinger didn't look too hopeful.

As Rhodes drove out of the parking lot, he looked back and saw both Skelly and Ballinger standing there, looking after him. It was hard to say which one of them looked the more depressed.

Chapter 2

As soon as he was out of the lot, Rhodes called Hack on the radio. He intended to stop somewhere to get a Dr Pepper if nothing was happening at the jail. Then he wanted to see what he could find out about the finances of Jack Storm. And, though he hated to think that someone like Ballinger could be involved in theft, he thought he should probably check on him and Skelly, too.

Things were not, however, going smoothly at the jail.

"You better get on back," Hack said. "Ruth's here, and she has a few things to tell you about."

Ruth meant Ruth Grady, one of Rhodes's deputies.

"What things?" Rhodes asked.

"Not things we want to talk about on the radio," Hack said.

Uh-oh, Rhodes thought. He could imagine all the scanner owners in the county wondering just what the heck was going on at the sheriff's office. Rhodes didn't blame them. He was wondering, too. He headed for the jail. When he got there, Ruth Grady was talking to Hack. Their relationship had improved considerably since she had come to the department.

Hack had been a little reluctant to accept a female deputy at first.

"What's the trouble?" Rhodes asked. He walked over to sit in his swivel chair, which no longer squeaked, thanks to Ruth's application of WD-40.

"It's kind of a long story," Ruth said. She was short and stout and in Rhode's opinion an excellent deputy. Maybe he was prejudiced, considering who she had replaced, but he didn't think so. It was true that Johnny Sherman had been something of a disgrace to the department, but Ruth had more than proved her worth, and she would have been an asset to anyone's law-enforcement operation.

"I've already heard one of those today," Rhodes said. "I guess another one wouldn't hurt anything."

"Something funny going on down at the funeral home?" Hack said.

Rhodes could tell that the old man was curious, but when he thought about all the times that Hack had made him wait to hear a story, he decided not to tell anything yet.

"I'll tell you later," Rhodes said. "You first," he said to Ruth.

"Well," Hack said, "I got this call while you were out—"

Rhodes looked at Ruth. "I thought you were the one with the story."

She grinned. "Hack has part of it, too. Maybe he ought to start."

Now he's got her doing it, Rhodes thought, but he didn't say anything. It would only encourage them.

"Yeah, I ought to start," Hack said when he saw that Rhodes wasn't going to stop him. "I got this call while you were out, from old lady McGee out at the lake."

"Which old lady McGee is that?" Rhodes asked.

"Sammie," Ruth said. "She lives out at the lake since her husband died. His name was Ferris."

"Ever'body called him Fibber," Hack said. He looked at Ruth. "I bet you don't know why."

"Sure I do," Ruth said. "They used to call everybody Fibber if his last name was McGee. It was because of some old guy on the radio. He had a closet that was so full he never wanted to open it."

Rhodes could tell that Hack was impressed. "I didn't think you'd be old enough to remember that," Hack said.

"I'm not," Ruth told him. "I heard about it from my grandfather."

Hack looked miffed. "Well, anyway, that's what they called him. He bought one of those lots out at the lake back in the fifties, before the dang things got so high that nobody could afford 'em. He was always goin' to move out there, but he never did. So after he died, his wife decided that she'd go. They had a couple of kids, but neither one of 'em stayed around here. I think the boy is out in California—"

"Wait a minute," Rhodes said. "What's her family history got to do with this?" He hated to interrupt Hack, but he was afraid they'd never get to the point of the story.

"Nothin', I guess," Hack said. "I just thought you might be interested in hearin' about it."

"I am," Rhodes said. "Just not right now."

"Humpf," Hack said, and turned back to his radio.

"She called in right after you left for Ballinger's," Ruth said, "or about then. Hack told me you'd just left. She wanted to report some prowlers."

"Out at the lake?" Rhodes said.

"That's right. Her husband built a little house out there right after he bought the property, and that's where she's living. There's quite a little community, but it's pretty deserted a lot of the time. People build houses out there and then live in them on the weekends."

Hack turned back to them. "Most of those folks ain't even from the county. Most of 'em are from Houston or Dallas, and they just come down here to fish or hunt."

"That's part of the problem," Ruth said. "To get to the place, you have to turn off the highway and go down that gravel road that winds back around the far side of the lake and then go across the dam. It's a pretty little area, but there are a lot of trees. It's hard to see one house from another one, and there's hardly ever anybody around."

13

Rhodes knew what she was getting at. "The houses are vulnerable to break-ins," he said.

"That's right. And Mrs. McGee thought someone was doing just that—breaking in."

"What made her think so?"

"It mighta been the moving van," Hack said. "That's usually a pretty good clue." Hack was still mad at being interrupted and also at being compared to Ruth's grandfather.

"What moving van?" Rhodes said.

"I was coming to that," Ruth said. "For the last couple of days, there's been a moving van traveling around some of the roads out there. She's seen it twice."

Rhodes was familiar with the area she was describing. "Those roads are pretty twisty and narrow for a moving van," he said.

"I don't think she really meant it was like a Mayflower Truck," Ruth said. "She described it to me as being more like one of those rental jobs. Green and white, with a pack mule painted on it."

"I've seen those," Rhodes said. " 'U-Truck-'Em.' "

"That's the one."

"So she's afraid some of the homes may have been burglarized." Rhodes had it figured out now. "Did you check any of them or just talk to her?"

"I thought I might need more than just her suspicion to enter a home," Ruth said.

"She needed to talk to somebody with authority," Hack said.

Rhodes ignored him. "All right. Let's drive on out there and have a look around. There's no need to start calling the owners and getting them all excited until we check it out. It might be that someone's just moving into a home out there." He looked at Hack. "If you need us, you know where we'll be."

"That's right," he said. "I sure know where you'll be."

The lake wasn't at its best in January. In the summer, the tall pecan trees were green and thick with leaves, but now

14

their branches were stark and black. The water was a muddy brown, and most of the aquatic vegetation had disappeared from its surface. Though the day was relatively warm, the water did not look as inviting as it often did to Rhodes, who sometimes contemplated what life might be like if he had a bass boat and the time to use it. He had often wanted to cruise along the shore, guiding his course with a trolling motor, and fish some of the minuscule coves, drag a lure beside some of the submerged tree stumps or try a topwater near the riprap of the dam. But not today. The bare trees, the muddy water, and the barren shoreline had no appeal for him.

They drove across the dam and down a winding gravel road. The houses were set back in the trees. Though you could see one from another, even without leaves, the trees pretty much obscured the view. He wondered why anyone like Sammie McGee would want to live out here all alone.

"Did Mrs. McGee have any idea where that truck might've been going or where it might have come from?"

"Maybe you ought to talk to her," Ruth said. "She lives right down here."

She turned the car into a gravel drive, and Rhodes could see the house through the tree trunks. It was small, built up off the ground on thick pilings in case the lake ever flooded, and had a porch running all along the front.

"That's her, sitting on the porch," Ruth said.

High, thin clouds had begun to mar the blue of the sky, but there was still plenty of sun. Rhodes saw a figure sitting in a chair in a patch of sunlight. Despite the unseasonably warm temperature, the figure was swathed in several layers of clothing. Ruth stopped the car near the porch, and she and Rhodes got out.

"Hello, again, Mrs. McGee," Ruth said, as they climbed the steps and walked down to where the old woman sat. "I brought the sheriff out to talk to you."

Mrs. McGee looked up at Rhodes from her seat in the chair. She had a crocheted afghan, red and blue and black, wrapped around her, and she was wearing a red knit cap

15

pulled down low on her forehead. She had watery blue eyes and thick jowls that quivered when she spoke.

"I hope you can do something about this, Sheriff," she said. "I'm just sure that something bad's going on around here."

"Why is that, Mrs. McGee?" Rhodes said.

"I've been sittin' out here on my porch, seein' that truck," she said. "Nobody around here's got a truck like that. Somebody's up to no good."

"Have you seen the truck stop at anyone's house?" Rhodes asked. He looked around. He could see only the top of one other house through the trees.

"Nope," she said. "Can't see that good. But I've seen it on the road. What else would a movin' truck be doin' out here?"

"We'll have a look around, then," Rhodes said. He was thinking that the old woman was just jumpy, as who wouldn't be, living out here practically in isolation like she was. Still, it wouldn't hurt to have a look.

"We'll let you know if we find anything," he said.

"You do that," the old woman said. "Not that it worries me."

She lifted the afghan and gave Rhodes a glimpse of what looked like an old Frontier model Colt's .44. He couldn't be sure; she dropped the afghan back too quickly for him to get a good look.

"I can take care of myself," she said. "I just like to know what I'm up against."

When they got back in the car, Ruth said, "Admit it. You were feeling sorry for the poor, defenseless old lady."

"You knew she had that cannon, didn't you?" Rhodes said.

Ruth laughed. "She showed it to me earlier. I didn't think to mention it. I think she knows how to handle it."

"She probably does," Rhodes said. "I don't guess we have to worry about her as much as we do anybody who tries to sneak up on her."

"That's the truth," Ruth said. "I wouldn't want to try it."

They drove to the house whose top Rhodes had been able

to catch sight of from Mrs. McGee's porch. Although it wasn't more than a city block from her property as the crow flies, they had to drive back to the road and turn down another drive to get to it. The mailbox said, The Washburn's.

"I never could figure out why people use apostrophes like that," Ruth said.

"Maybe they want to let you know that somebody named Washburn owns that mailbox," Rhodes said.

They parked in front of the house and Rhodes got out. The drive was covered in fallen leaves, and he kicked through them as he went to the front door. This house was a small wooden-frame structure, no larger than Mrs. McGee's and not built up on pilings as hers had been. Either the Washburns had more confidence that the area wouldn't flood or they had better flood insurance.

There were two steps up to the door. Brown leaves lay on them almost as thickly as on the drive. Rhodes knocked, but he was sure no one was there. The owners might not have cleared the drive if they had been in residence, but surely they would have knocked the leaves off the steps. Also, there was no car to be seen.

No answer came to Rhodes's knock. The door had rattled loosely in its frame. He looked at it, then tried the knob. The door was unlocked.

Rhodes went back to the car. "Call Hack," he said. "Let him know where we are and tell him we're going inside." He went back to the house and opened the door, letting it swing inward.

He stepped through and looked around. He was standing in what was obviously the living room or den. He couldn't tell which one for sure because there was no furniture. In fact, the room was completely bare. There were no pictures on the walls, no chairs or couch, no carpeting on the floor.

Ruth Grady came into the room behind Rhodes. He glanced back to see that she had her .38 drawn and ready. He didn't object. She had gotten him out of more than one bad situation where he had gone in carelessly or too quickly.

"Looks like they moved out," she said.

"Maybe," Rhodes said.

They went through the entire house. It didn't take long. There was one other large room—a bedroom probably—a bathroom, and a kitchen. All of them were as bare as the first room had been. There hadn't even been any medicine in the cabinet in the bathroom, though Rhodes had noticed a roll of toilet tissue sitting beside the commode. In the kitchen there was a length of copper pipe sticking out from the wall, the end crimped.

"Looks like they had an icemaker on the refrigerator," Ruth said. She had holstered her pistol and was looking curiously around the room. "Wonder why they didn't just cut off the water?"

"There's no cutoff in here," Rhodes said. "It must be outside. Maybe it was too much trouble."

"Maybe they didn't move out, either," Ruth said.

"Let's hope they did," Rhodes said. "We'd better check another house or two."

The next house belonged to the Clayton's.

"There must have been a mailbox painter who gave them a special deal," Ruth said as she steered the car down the winding drive.

The Claytons had a better location than either the Washburns or Mrs. McGee. Their house backed up right on the water, and there was a sturdy-looking wooden pier running out into the water. The house was built of rough-cut boards and had a much more impressive facade than the others. The drive and front yard were strewn with leaves. Rhodes could tell as soon as he stepped out of the car that the front door was open. It was swung about halfway back into the house.

"Call Hack," he said.

The house was as bare as the other one had been. This refrigerator had had an icemaker, too, and again the end of the copper tubing was neatly crimped.

"Looks like everybody's moving out," Ruth said. She kept looking around. "The only difference in this place and the other one is the smell."

Rhodes had noticed the smell, too. "Maybe an animal died under the house," he said.

Ruth looked at him. "You think that's what it is—something dead?"

Rhodes was sure. It was the kind of odor you never forgot once you had smelled it. "Did we look everywhere in here?"

"I think so. The closets and everywhere. There was nothing in them."

As they stood there, the odor seemed to get stronger. "What about that door over there?" Rhodes said.

"That looks like a pantry," Ruth said. "Or maybe that's where the hot-water heater is."

"I guess we'd better check it," Rhodes said.

He didn't want to, but he walked over and put his hand on the knob. The odor seemed stronger than ever, but he told himself that it was just his imagination. He turned the knob and opened the door. If he hadn't stepped aside, the mummy would have hit him as it fell into the room.

It wasn't really a mummy, of course, though Rhodes's first thought had been of Boris Karloff chasing after Zita Johann. This was even worse—a real human being, or what had once been a human being, completely wrapped up in silver duct tape.

The duct tape had broken in a few places where the pressure of the gases in the body had been too much for it. That was the source of most of the smell. The color of the viscous fluids on the outside of the tape was too much for Rhodes to take in, and he looked away. He could still hear the plopping sound the mummy had made as it hit the floor. Several strands of tape had burst at that moment, releasing more of the odor into the room.

When Rhodes turned back, trying not to breathe too deeply, Ruth Grady was kneeling down examining the body, or what she could see of it. "Hard to tell even if it's a man or a woman," she said.

Rhodes wondered how she could be so calm. He could feel his own heart beating a mile a minute, and he promised himself a session on the exercise bike as soon as he got home. He hadn't been riding regularly lately, and he was really out of shape. He knew that being out of shape had nothing at all to do with the way he was feeling however.

19

"You go call Hack," he said to Ruth. "Get him to send an ambulance and the JP for this district."

Mrs. McGee had been right, he thought. Something bad was going on around there.

Chapter 3

RHODES COULD REMEMBER when there hadn't been a Clearview Lake.

He stood on the pier behind the house and looked out over the muddy water. There was a huge bank of dark blue, almost purple clouds building in the north, and he knew that the norther he had been thinking about earlier would be blowing through any time now. Already the wind was kicking up a little, and the water was slapping gently against the pilings of the pier.

The lake had been built more than thirty years before by damming the river that flowed through the southwestern part of the county. Rhodes supposed it had been a project of the Corps of Engineers, but he didn't remember for sure. The lake had become a part of the county's everyday life since then—a place for picnics, fishing, and boating. A few people lived here, but most of them, as Hack had observed, were not residents of the nearby towns. They lived in the city during the week and visited the lake on Saturdays and Sundays, or made it a sort of summer home-away-from-home.

The locals had become so familiar with the place that they

had dropped the first part of the name. To them it was just the lake. Nobody called it anything else, not even after the big county lake had been built by the power companies down below Thurston.

As far as Rhodes could remember there had never been any trouble at the lake. The county cars made it part of their regular patrol, but there had never been any reason to pay it special attention. After thirty years, people could get a little lax, but it was too late to worry about that now. He walked back toward the Clayton house, the sound of his heels hollow on the boards of the pier.

Dr. White had come, along with the ambulance crew and the JP. Rhodes was glad that Hack had thought to notify the doctor. Ruth hadn't specified the problem over the radio, but Hack had known what the trouble was from her request for an ambulance and justice of the peace. Those two things almost always added up to a death of one kind or another.

Dr. White hadn't liked the scene. Peeling the tape off the body was going to be a truly messy job, and there wasn't going to be any possibility of identification from physical features. Rhodes didn't particularly want to think about what the person under the tape looked like.

He stepped onto the lake shore. Most of the work in the house had been done, the measurements made, the time and circumstances recorded. Ruth Grady was taking a last look around in case they had missed anything the first time, though Rhodes didn't think that likely.

Now came the hard part. Checking out the other houses in the area to see how many of them had been burgled, notifying the owners, and trying to figure out just who the body was—or had been.

There was no county morgue. Dr. White did his work at Ballinger's and that was where Rhodes found him.

"The body was that of a well-nourished white female, about thirty-five years of age," Dr. White said.

Rhodes had noticed that in the last few years, Dr. White had begun to talk like an autopsy report.

"Any clothing? Any identification? Anything at all to tell us who she was?" Rhodes asked.

"Nothing. She was completely nude." The old doctor shook his head. "I tell you, Sheriff, I never saw anything like it. When I peeled the tape back, her skin . . . Never mind. Let's just say that I won't be able to talk to you about any identifying marks."

Rhodes could imagine what the body must have looked like. "That's all right," he said.

"I didn't really look for them," Dr. White said. "After the first few rounds of tape peeling, well, I didn't peel anymore. I just cut through it as if it were the skin."

"How did she die? Any idea?"

"Oh, yes. That's the easy part. She was shot. I have the bullet for you. It looks like a .38."

They were sitting in Ballinger's office, surrounded by books with titles like *Scream Bloody Murder*, *The Killer Inside Me*, and *Some of Your Blood*. It was an appropriate place, Rhodes thought, but he wondered just how many people Ballinger allowed in there. There were a lot of folks in Clearview who might not have understood their funeral director's reading habits.

"One shot?" Rhodes said.

"In the right temple. Massive trauma to the brain. She must have died instantly."

"And then someone wrapped her in duct tape and put her in a closet."

"Not exactly," Dr. White told him. "At least I would say not."

"What, then?"

"From the way that blood had been pooled in her buttocks and legs, I would say that she had been lying in a reclining position for quite some time before being placed in the closet. At least if your impression is correct."

"What impression?"

"That the body was standing in the closet and fell forward as you opened the door."

"That's the way it happened, all right. How long would you say that she's been dead?"

23

"A difficult question," Dr. White said, "and one that brings up another question. Why the tape?"

"I'd been wondering about that," Rhodes said.

"I can only speculate, of course," Dr. White said.

"I'll settle for that."

"All right. I can't really give you a very good estimate of the time of death. The main problem is the tape. Did you happen to notice how tightly it was wrapped around the body?"

"I noticed," Rhodes said.

"It might have been done that way to slow down decomposition," Dr. White said. "No air could get to the body, or at least certainly not as much air as if the body had been exposed completely. The tape may also have slowed down the usual bacteria."

"So what's your best guess?"

"I prefer to call it an estimate," Dr. White said.

"Estimate, then."

"It's been unusually warm lately, the body was inside. I'd say three weeks. Approximately."

"I won't hold you to it," Rhodes said. He thanked Dr. White and went back to the jail.

Ruth Grady had finished getting in touch with the owners of most of the houses. She and Rhodes found five others that had been entered and stripped of everything that could be carried away. They also talked to the homeowners who lived there. None of them had noticed anything out of the ordinary, and none of them had seen the U-Truck-'Em van.

"This is really something," Hack said after Rhodes filled them in on Dr. White's report. He had forgotten his earlier irritation. "Looked just like a mummy, huh?"

"That's right," Rhodes said. "What about the Claytons, Ruth?"

"They're the only ones I haven't been able to contact," she said. "All the others will be here this afternoon or tomorrow to check on their property. It's going to be really crowded around here."

24

Rhodes wasn't looking forward to that. "We've got to get to the Claytons. The corpse was in their house."

"I'll keep trying," she said. "It's not easy to find people on the weekends. I'm surprised that none of them were down here at the lake."

"Not the right kind of weather," Hack said. "I bet they all wish they'd been coming up every week to check on their houses, though."

"You know who's going to get the blame for that," Rhodes said.

Hack smiled. "That's why they pay you a big salary," he said.

"Sure it is. And there's something else we have to worry about." He told them about the robbery of the corpse at the funeral home.

"Now who would do a thing like that?" Hack said.

"Exactly what I'd like to know," Rhodes said. "You heard any gossip about Skelly or Ballinger being in financial trouble?"

"Now surely you don't think one of those old boys would rob corpses."

"No, I don't. But I don't know who else would, either."

Lawton came in through the doorway leading to the cell area. "Who else would do what?" he said.

He had a smooth, round face, and Rhodes had always thought he resembled the comedian Lou Costello. In fact, Rhodes thought that Hack resembled Bud Abbott and that when Hack and Lawton got together vaudeville lived again. He was never sure that their routines were practiced, but he often suspected they were.

"We were talkin' about what happened over at the funeral home," Hack said, then explained to Lawton, more or less straightforwardly, what had occurred.

"Wouldn't neither of those two fellas do a thing like that," Lawton said.

Ruth Grady hung up the phone. "I still can't contact anyone," she said. "Do you want me to get in touch with the police department?"

25

"Good idea," Rhodes told her. "Have them notify Clayton and ask them to have him get in touch with us."

She turned back to the phone. Rhodes could hear her dialing.

"They got people cleaning up over there at Ballinger's," Lawton said. "You talk to them?"

Rhodes had to admit he hadn't. He wondered why Ballinger hadn't thought of that himself, instead of suggesting Skelly. "I'll get on it," he said.

"You'd think a man in a high-payin' job like his would've thought of that," Lawton said to Hack.

Hack was feeling generous. "It would've come to him, but he's got bigger things on his mind."

Rhodes knew Hack was willing to excuse him, then let him off the hook so easily because no one had told Lawton about the dead woman in the cabin. Neither Hack nor Lawton liked to be the last to find out anything that happened around the office, and each one delighted in getting ahead of the other. Now Hack would feel one up on Lawton for days, or until something else happened that Lawton found out about first.

While Hack told his story with relish, Rhodes turned back to Ruth Grady.

"They're going to notify Clayton," she said. "I talked to an Officer Ferguson. She said she'd take care of it. I didn't know those Dallas police were so nice."

"Is she going to tell him about the body?"

"She'll leave that to us. She thinks she might know this Ted Clayton, though, and she's going to check on him for us, see if he has a record or something."

"If we had us one of them computers, we could do that for ourselves," Hack said. He had been agitating for a computer for several months. "We could just plug into the state and local networks and get all that information lickety-split."

"I've been talking to the commissioners," Rhodes said. "If the budget can stand it, we may get a computer this year."

"About time," Hack said.

Lawton wasn't saying anything. He was sulking. After a

26

few seconds he turned and went back into the cell area. "Gotta sweep up," he said over his shoulder as he slunk out.

Rhodes left Ruth Grady to deal with the property owners who would be coming in later in the day. He wanted to drive back out to the lake and look for signs of the rental van. It just might be that it was someone local and the van was parked right there in some garage or driveway. Ruth had already tried to check with the rental company. She was informed that the company had gone out of business six months before and all the vans sold at auction. The auction firm would forward a list of the buyers. There'd been a lot of them.

"Won't take long," Hack had said. "They'll prob'ly just punch it up on their computer and print it right out."

Rhodes wondered just when Hack had learned so much about computers, and if Hack knew as much about computers as he seemed to think he did. Rhodes also hoped that when and if the commissioners came through with the money he wouldn't have to be the one who learned to use it. He wasn't sure he could, in spite of Hack's assurances that even little kids did it all the time. Still, it would be a real convenience if it worked out.

The wind was blowing hard now, and the temperature had dropped by at least twenty degrees. It would be down below freezing by nightfall. Rhodes drove around the shore of the lake, across the dam, and down among the houses that looked so deserted in the bare trees. The wind swirled the dead leaves in the road and scraped them across the windshield. Rhodes could see why the houses had appeared to be easy pickings to the burglars. They could come in the middle of the day and no one would notice. Still, he suspected that most of their work had been done at night. He had checked the patrol schedule, and the county cars went through every night, but only once—twice on Saturdays. Park the van behind the house and it would never be spotted. Park it in front and it might have been, but only *might*.

This driving around was getting him nowhere, so he pulled in at Mrs. McGee's. She was no longer sitting on the porch, which came as no surprise. In the mild temperature of the morning she had been wrapped up as if preparing for an expedition to the Arctic.

Rhodes stopped the car and got out. The raw wind whipped through his pants legs as if the material were fishnet, and gusted a piece of grit into his eye. He climbed up on the porch, turned his back to the wind, and rubbed until his eye teared up and washed out the tiny particle. He knocked on the door. When Mrs. McGee answered, he was greeted by a blast of heat that felt as if he had just opened the door of an oven.

"Come in, Sheriff," Mrs. McGee said. "Don't stand there and let all the heat out."

He stepped inside. The room was small and neat, the hardwood floor polished to a high gloss and the area rugs placed precisely in the right places. Rhodes wondered if a floor like that wasn't dangerous for an old woman, but he didn't say anything about it. Mrs. McGee, despite the heat in the room, was still dressed as she had been while sitting outside, the knit cap still pulled down on her brow.

"Come have a seat," she said. "No need to stand up."

There were a couple of old-fashioned rocking chairs pulled close to a Dearborn heater, which had been turned up about as high as it would go. The wooden arm of the chair Rhodes sat in was hot to the touch. He moved the chair back a bit and turned so that his legs would not get scorched. Mrs. McGee, on the other hand, drew herself closer.

"When you get old, your blood thins out," she said. "It gets harder to take the cold every year."

"I've heard that," Rhodes said, and he had. He wasn't quite sure that he believed it, though.

"You didn't come here to talk about an old woman's thin blood, I guess," she said. "Is it about those burglaries?"

"Yes," Rhodes said. He told her about the body in the Clayton house.

"Land alive," she said. "The world is gettin' to be a terrible place these days."

Rhodes agreed. "I just wanted to let you know that we'll be stepping up the patrols through this area. I don't think you have anything to worry about, since they've obviously been

28

avoiding houses where people are living, but I thought you ought to know about the dead woman.''

"I still got my gun," she said. "You don't have to worry about me. Fibber taught me how to use it before he died."

Rhodes hoped her husband had been a good teacher and wished the old woman didn't seem so eager to use her pistol. She might use it on the wrong person.

"Did you know the Claytons, by any chance?" he said.

"Never saw 'em," she said. "Folks out here aren't very sociable. I mostly sit on my porch or watch TV." She looked over to a corner of the room, where there was an old console color TV set with a rounded picture tube. Rhodes hadn't seen very many of those lately.

"You saw the moving van go by while you were outside?" he said.

"That's right. In the fall and winter I can see the road real good. I know a lot about who comes and goes around here."

"Didn't you think that van was an unusual sight?"

"Nope. You never can tell what you might see, and people move in and out all the time."

"You saw it during the day, though? Not at night?"

"I sit out on my porch a lot when it's pretty weather. But that's in the daytime, not at night. Sometimes in the summer I can sit out there till right past sunset, but it starts to get cool about that time and I have to come in."

There were days in the summer when the temperature in Blacklin County stayed in the nineties until ten o'clock in the evening or later, but Rhodes didn't think it was worth mentioning. Besides, he'd noticed that the room wasn't quite as warm as he'd first thought. The old house wasn't well insulated, and he could feel an occasional cold breath of air on the back of his neck. He was glad of that. It probably meant that at least Mrs. McGee wouldn't suffocate.

"So you wouldn't have seen the van if it came by here after dark?"

Mrs. McGee looked at Rhodes as if he were particularly stupid. "That's what I said."

"And you didn't hear anything out of the ordinary, like a gunshot?"

29

"I don't hear much that goes on when I'm in the house," she said. "I can hear that wind whinin' out there, but that's about all."

They both listened to the wind for a minute as it buffeted the house and whistled in the cracks.

"How do you like living out here?" Rhodes asked.

Mrs. McGee laughed. "What you mean is, why does an old woman like me want to live all the way out here by myself? Am I right?"

"I guess so," Rhodes said. He smiled sheepishly.

"Listen," she said. "I got me a good car parked out in the back, and I can go into town whenever I want to. Truth is, I don't want to much. Mostly I like to sit out here on my porch and look at things. Trees. Birds. Squirrels. Things like that. I like 'em a lot better than most of the people I see in town."

Rhodes had to admit she had a point. He told her to take care of herself and went back to town.

Chapter 4

WHEN RHODES WALKED into the jail, Lawton was looking almost happy, which Rhodes interpreted as a bad sign. The only thing that could have cheered Lawton up after his previous besting by Hack would be something that Rhodes wasn't going to like hearing about.

Hack was sitting by the radio. He turned when Rhodes walked in. Hack was smiling too, and Rhodes decided that Hack was going to let Lawton bring up the latest disaster in order to make up for what had occurred earlier. Though there was a form of competition between the two old men, they were really friends, and neither wanted the other to feel bad for long.

"All right," Rhodes said. "What is it?"

"You want the good news or the bad news?" Lawton said.

Rhodes knew for sure that he was in for it then. "Who's got the good news?" he said.

"I do," Lawton told him.

"All right," Rhodes said. "Let's have it."

Lawton pretended to look carefully around the office. "Ruth ain't around, is she?"

As a matter of fact she wasn't. Rhodes wondered where she might have gotten off to, but knew he would find out sooner or later.

"I don't see her," Rhodes said.

"Me neither," Hack said.

"I guess it's okay, then," Lawton said. "You remember that little item that got stolen from Dr. Packer's last week?"

Rhodes knew then why Lawton had made the show about looking for Ruth. There were certain things that neither he nor Hack liked to talk about in front of her, even if she had seen and experienced nearly everything that a law officer could. And that covered a lot of territory.

"The veterinarian's," Rhodes said. "It was an ejaculator."

Lawton looked around the room again. It was a small room, cluttered with three desks, six chairs, and a gun cabinet. There was no place where Ruth could have been hiding.

"That wasn't all they took," Lawton said.

"I know that," Rhodes said. "Mostly they took drugs. But that was what you were talking about, wasn't it?"

Hack interrupted before Lawton could answer. "I never could figure out just why a man would want to take drugs that were supposed to be used on horses or somethin'."

"Some of those drugs can affect humans in strange ways. Some of them are powerful aphrodisiacs, for instance. But never mind. What about that ejaculator?" Rhodes asked.

"They found it," Lawton said.

Rhodes waited patiently. He knew that both Lawton and Hack were hoping that he would ask who *they* were, but he was determined to wait them out. A minute passed before his nerve cracked.

"Who is this *they*?" he said.

"Miz Sunday's little girls, Suzanne and Sarah," Lawton said.

"Oh," Rhodes said.

"See," Hack said, "the way we figger it, the thief just took that thing because it was layin' around. He didn't know what it was or anything—"

He broke off. Lawton was glaring at him from across the room.

"Uh, anyway," Hack said. "Never mind."

Lawton picked up the theory. "He didn't know what it was or anything, so he just chucked it out when he was drivin' down the road. It landed in the bar ditch in front of Miz Sunday's house, and that's where those two little girls found it."

"How old are the little girls?" Rhodes said.

"Suzanne must be eleven now," Lawton said. "Little Sarah's about eight."

"So they probably didn't know what it was any more than the thief did," Rhodes said.

"Maybe not," Lawton said, "but their mama sure did. She was brought up on a farm, and she was mighty upset that a 'jaculator had wound up in a bar ditch in front of her house, I'll tell you."

"Is that where Ruth went?"

"Yep," Lawton said. "I ain't at all sure it's right, her pickin' up evidence like that. I mean . . . well . . ."

"She'll be all right," Rhodes said. "Did any of those homeowners come by yet?"

"Not yet," Hack said. "I guess you'll have to deal with 'em if they show up now."

"And that's the bad news," Rhodes said.

"No," Hack said. "That's not the bad news."

Rhodes hadn't really thought so. He had hoped so, though. "Okay," he said. "Tell me the bad news, then."

"That Officer Ferguson called back from Dallas," Hack said.

Rhodes waited. This time he was determined not to be the one to speak first.

Hack finally gave in. Being second had made him less patient than Lawton. "She said they knew about that Clayton fella, all right." He paused again and waited.

Rhodes waited too.

Hack relented. "He didn't have a record, but he'd been in to the station before."

This time Rhodes didn't wait. "Why?" he said.

"It was about his wife," Hack said. "Seems he turned in a missing persons report on her."

Somehow, Rhodes wasn't surprised. "When was that?"

"January second," Hack said.

Exactly three weeks before. Dr. White would be pleased, Rhodes thought.

The door of the jail swung open, and the wind grabbed it, swinging it hard into the wall. A fat man about five feet six inches tall stood in the doorway. "What's this about my house being robbed out at the lake?" he demanded.

Rhodes sighed. It was time to deal with the public again.

When Rhodes got home it was after six o'clock. Speedo, his dog, whose real name was Mr. Earl, was in the backyard, waiting patiently to be fed. The cold weather didn't bother Speedo much. In fact, he seemed to enjoy it. Rhodes got the bag of Old Roy out and fed him, then went into the house.

He walked into the living room, where the TV set was. Sitting on top of it was the brand new VCR that Ivy Daniel had given him for Christmas. He had often thought about buying one, but never had. He liked to tell himself that old movies, the kind he preferred to watch, were best viewed at the time of night the TV stations deigned to show them.

Now he knew that he had been kidding himself. He hadn't bought a VCR because he had a fear of technology, which if he were going to be honest about it was probably also the reason he had never really pushed the county commissioners about the computer that Hack seemed to think was such a necessity. It was a foolish fear. Rhodes had learned to program the VCR with very little difficulty, and the night before he had taped one of his favorite old movies, *White Heat*.

There was one problem. It was a colorized version. He wondered if his dislike of the coloring of black-and-white movies was another example of his fear of technology, but he didn't think so. He just didn't think they looked very good. He had to admit that one he had seen, *The Charge of the Light Brigade*, hadn't been too bad, but he wasn't sure about *White Heat*. Still, there was a chance that the last scene, where the oil refinery blows up, might be really spectacular in color.

Ivy was coming over to watch it with him, and he suddenly remembered that there was nothing to eat in the house. That is, there was nothing if you didn't count the bologna in the refrigerator, and Ivy wouldn't count that. She was constantly trying to get him to do something about his diet, but somehow he never seemed to have the time to put together a proper meal.

Then it occurred to him that not only had he not bought anything for supper, he hadn't eaten lunch, either. He realized that he was very hungry and wondered how it was that a man who hardly ever seemed to eat, and who was on the go most of the time, could develop a stomach that was beginning to bulge over his belt.

The bicycle. He had promised himself he would do a few rounds on the exercise bike, but there wasn't time now. He had to go out and find something to fix for supper in a short time. Ivy would be here by seven-thirty.

Rhodes got in his own pickup, preferring not to take the county car to the grocery store. It wasn't that anyone would say anything about it; he just didn't think it was a good idea. Speedo wanted to go, so Rhodes let down the tailgate. The dog took a running start and jumped in the pickup bed. Rhodes slammed the tailgate shut. Speedo liked to put his front feet up on the side of the bed and hang his head over in the wind. Why even a dog would want to do that on a day like this one, Rhodes couldn't figure out.

Rhodes drove to the big Brookshire Brothers store and parked in the lot. He left Speedo in the pickup. There was a large sign in the store's front window that said, "No Dogs Allowed except Seeing-Eye Dogs." As far as Rhodes knew, there wasn't a single seeing-eye dog in all of Blacklin County, but there the sign was anyway.

Rhodes went into the store. He didn't mind grocery shopping, though he was told that most men hated it. He simply never had time to do it; and when he did, only enough time to pick up something easy to fix, like bologna. Bologna didn't require much fixing.

He picked out a couple of steaks and some potatoes to bake. He wasn't very good at salads, but he got a head of lettuce. Put a little salad dressing on it, and it would do. He hoped.

Outside, once more, the wind felt even colder. It was going to be a really cold night. He hoped Speedo would be comfortable in his barrel and wondered if there was enough straw in it.

Rhodes drove home slowly, thinking about the murdered woman. This was a case almost without clues. All he had was a .38 bullet. The house had been as clean as a preacher's plate. Whoever was taking everything out of those places was extremely neat about it.

The lack of clues in itself didn't bother Rhodes much. He worked a lot more on his instincts than on clues, for one thing. He liked to talk to people and keep talking to them, until things began to come together. One of the problems in this case so far was that there wasn't really anybody to talk to, except for Mrs. McGee, and she didn't appear to know anything. You could never be sure about something like that, though. Rhodes would talk to her again. Sometimes people knew more than they thought they knew, or more then *you* thought they knew.

He got home, romped around the yard with Speedo for a minute, then took the food in. It was too cold and windy to spend any more time outside than absolutely necessary.

He turned on the oven, ran the steaks under the broiler, washed the potatoes, and wrapped them in foil. He stuck them in the oven with the steaks. It was his theory that you couldn't cook either a steak or a potato too much. He would fix the salad after Ivy got there. He hoped he had time to wash up and get ready.

He was worried about the dead woman, too. There didn't seem to be much doubt about who she was, and when Ruth had come back with the ejaculator he had asked her to call Dallas and have them find Ted Clayton as soon as possible. Clayton was someone Rhodes wanted very much to talk to.

Also, he had begun to wonder just how long the burglars had been operating around the lake. He supposed it was possible that they had been in the area for quite some time. The fact that no one had reported the truck meant very little. After all, it appeared to be just a normal rental truck, and for all Rhodes knew, it was. He put out the word to the other deputies to be on the look-out for it, however.

As he was combing his hair, he heard a knock on the door. It was just as well. He had been standing there for at least two minutes, wondering if there weren't a lot more hair in the comb than usual. He hoped he wasn't going to start losing his hair. It was bad enough that he couldn't seem to control his weight.

He went to the door and let Ivy in. She looked very pretty to him, with her short, graying hair and her bright smile. He wondered why it was that on her, gray hair looked good. He was afraid that his own would turn that dirty yellow color that seemed to plague so many men.

Ivy was wearing jeans and a Western shirt, and on the third finger of her left hand was the emerald ring that Rhodes had bought her for Christmas. The emerald had been a big disappointment to Hack and Lawton, both of whom had been thinking that Rhodes would buy her a diamond, but at least it was a ring. They would probably have killed him if he hadn't given her a ring. Since both he and Ivy had been married before, he somehow felt that an emerald was more appropriate than a diamond. She had told him that she was having her other rings made into a dinner ring.

Now that they were more or less officially engaged, at least in the eyes of the jail staff, Rhodes had been thinking very seriously of marriage—something that he realized he had been trying to avoid thinking about throughout most of his relationship with Ivy. Actually, he had thought of it, but mostly in a negative way. It was beginning to seem more and more like a good idea to him, however.

"What's that smell?" Ivy said as she came in the door.

"Steaks," Rhodes said. "I'm broiling some steaks and baking a couple of potatoes."

"Let's check on them," Ivy said.

Rhodes followed her into the kitchen, where she rescued

the potatoes and flipped over the steaks. "Shouldn't be too much longer," she said.

"I like mine well done," Rhodes said.

"So do I," Ivy told him, "but it still won't be long."

"Good," Rhodes said. "I'll fix the salad." He got the lettuce out of the refrigerator, quartered it, and set two of the quarters on salad plates. "Lettuce wedges," he said, getting a jar of salad dressing from the refrigerator. He always had salad dressing because he liked to spread it on the bread when he made bologna sandwiches.

"They may be a little too big," Ivy said. She got the knife and cut each of the wedges in half, returning the rest to the refrigerator.

Rhodes rummaged around, looking for steak knives, finally finding them in the back of a drawer. He wasn't comfortable in domestic situations, and he hoped that Ivy would offer to set the table. He was never sure which side of the plate to put the forks on. Unfortunately, she didn't offer. She was busy checking on the steaks, so Rhodes set the plates and put out the silverware. He hoped he got it right.

The steaks turned out to be very good, done just the way Rhodes liked them—no pink on the inside, but not completely dried out the way he usually cooked them when he had the nerve to try. It was probably a good thing Ivy had come when she did.

While they ate, he told her about the missing jewelry at the funeral home and the burglaries at the lake. He also told her about the dead woman. He had gotten into the habit of discussing his cases with her, and in fact she had been very helpful to him more than once. She was a good listener and often made good suggestions. She even helped him interview witnesses on occasion.

"What do you think?" she said. "The Clayton woman caught the thieves in the act and they killed her?"

"It's possible," Rhodes said, trying to deal with his lettuce wedge. "They're the kind who don't leave any loose ends, that's for sure. Those houses look like they've been gone over by a vacuum cleaner. That's how clean they are.

Whoever cleaned them out even crimped the ends of the copper tubing that attached to the refrigerator ice-makers.''

"You have any ideas about who did it?''

Ivy took a drink of ice water. Rhodes would have preferred Dr Pepper—he hadn't had one all day—but he thought it might look bad to have Dr Pepper with a meal, so he was drinking water, too.

"None,'' he said. "We're going to get a printout of the names of people who bought those trucks, but I don't know how much that will help, unless of course it turns out that someone who lives right around here is on the list. That would narrow it down. And of course I'll talk to Clayton. He might have some information for us.''

"Is he a suspect?''

"When a wife is murdered, the husband is always a suspect,'' Rhodes said. "Hard to believe he'd just stash her right there in his own house, though.''

"What about the problem at Ballinger's?''

Rhodes shook his head. "That one really bothers me. I'd think it was just the family trying to cash in if Tom Skelly hadn't told me that he put the jewelry on Mrs. Storm himself. I've got to talk to the people who work there, cleaning up and so on. I'm convinced that Tom and Clyde wouldn't take anything, no matter what it was.''

"I don't know,'' Ivy said. "That Clyde Ballinger has pretty strange reading habits. I remember that time I was in his office, and some of those books of his were very unusual. *Guerrilla Girls* was one of them. And he reads a lot of mystery novels. Maybe he got the idea from one of them.''

She had just about finished her steak and potato. Rhodes noticed that she ate the skin of the potato, and he was glad. He thought that was the best part, himself.

"He may read those things, but they don't give him any ideas,'' Rhodes said. "Except that he thinks we ought to be solving crimes down here in Blacklin County the same way they do in somewhere called Isola.''

"Isola?''

"It's a place in those books he reads. It's a lot like New York City.''

"And he thinks we ought to be like that?"

"Not exactly. He just admires the crime-fighting efficiency of the police force there." Rhodes did, too, for that matter. He had read one of the books himself, and he thought it wouldn't be bad to be as good as the men of the 87th. Or the eight-seven, as they probably called it.

"I think you do just fine," Ivy said. "Is there any dessert?"

Rhodes hadn't thought about dessert. "Uh, no," he said. "I'm trying to watch my weight."

Ivy laughed as she got up from the table. "I don't know why you worry about that so much. You look just fine."

Rhodes sneaked a downward glance. He couldn't see his belt buckle, but there wasn't really that much of an overhang, he guessed. Besides, he was sitting down, and that always made him kind of spread out more than was really natural.

He stood up and started to gather up the plates.

"If you treat me right, I might give you a hand with the dishes," Ivy said.

Rhodes was grateful for her help. He was generally pretty clumsy with plates and glasses, yet another reason why he preferred bologna sandwiches. You could eat them off a paper towel or a napkin and not feel bad about it. In fact, they were better if you ate them that way.

It didn't take long to get things squared away, but Rhodes dreaded the job of cleaning the oven. He didn't often broil anything, and when he did, it seemed to make a big mess, what with all the popping and splattering. He made a firm resolution to stick to sandwiches as much as possible.

He washed and Ivy dried. When everything was put away, they went in to watch the movie.

Rhodes turned off the timer and pushed the rewind button.

"What's this one about?" Ivy said. She was perfectly willing to watch the movies with him, but she'd not heard of most of them before. Neither she nor her late husband had been movie buffs.

"James Cagney plays a gangster," Rhodes said. "Goes to prison, breaks out. He has this thing for his mother."

"You're kidding?" Ivy said as she made herself comfortable on the couch. "James Cagney?"

"That's right. It's pretty good, though. This is the colorized version. I kind of want to see how the ending looks."

It didn't look very good at all. The color was so washed out that in fact the ending would have been more spectacular in the original black and white. Rhodes was very disappointed.

He didn't consider the evening a total loss, however. No evening spent on the couch with Ivy Daniel could ever be called that.

Chapter 5

RHODES ALWAYS WENT DOWN to the jail on Sunday mornings to check on things. Saturday nights brought in an assortment of inmates picked up on charges ranging from creating a disturbance to DWI. Most of the offenses were minor, and most of the offenders would see the judge on Monday, pay a fine, and go home.

The jail was hardly ever crowded, except on Sundays, a situation that had led the governor to consider paying the smaller counties to house prisoners for some of the larger ones. Those large jails were filled to overflowing because the Texas Department of Corrections didn't have room in the prison units for any more prisoners. As a result, prisoners were being released from the TDC units with some regularity, just to take in new offenders. Some criminals were serving very short sentences, and citizens were complaining. No matter how much they complained, however, Rhodes hoped he wouldn't have to be taking in prisoners from places like Harris or Dallas. His jail wasn't equipped for it, and neither was his staff.

It was a bad day to be in jail, if there ever could be a good one. The sky was thickly overcast, and the gunmetal clouds seemed almost low enough to touch. The temperature was in the high twenties and not likely to get any higher, which meant that the cells would be unpleasantly cool. The wind was still blowing hard and would be screeching through the cracks and crevices, of which there were plenty.

Hack, however, looked fairly comfortable. He was wearing an old gray pullover sweater with holes in the front, either torn or eaten by moths, Rhodes wasn't sure which, and a red-and-black plaid flannel shirt.

"Anything exciting going on?" Rhodes asked.

"Not much," Hack answered. "We had the usual run last night, nothin' special to speak of. Nothin' we needed to bother you about."

Rhodes thought he detected the hint of a smile with the last sentence, but he wasn't sure. It wasn't worth commenting on, anyway.

Rhodes went to his desk and read through most of the reports. Nothing seemed to warrant any special attention, though there had been a domestic disturbance that could have turned nasty. Then he went through the stack of reports filed by the owners of the homes at the lake, concentrating on the descriptions of stolen property. One of the men, Miles Emmit, had been more thorough than the others. He had brought with him Polaroid prints of most of the items that had been in his house. Rhodes paid special attention to those things that he might recognize later—a .44 Colt's revolver with checkered grips, a VCR with a wired remote. He was going through the photos when the phone rang.

It was Clyde Ballinger. "You caught those thieves yet?" he asked.

Rhodes didn't have to ask which thieves he meant. "No," he said. "Who do you have cleaning up over there?"

"We can talk about that when you get here," Ballinger said. "It's happened again."

Ballinger and Tom Skelly were in Ballinger's office when Rhodes got there. "I just can't figure it out," Ballinger said.

"You try to run an honest business, you do the best you can, and this is what you get—ripped off."

"Who is it this time?" Rhodes said.

"Mrs. Minnie West," Skelly said.

"I don't think I know her," Rhodes said.

"Lived out in Milsby. Her husband's Woody West," Skelly said.

Rhodes didn't know him either.

"Never mind that," Ballinger said. "Tell him what happened."

"She came in Friday night," Skelly said. "In fact, she was in the Blessed Assurance room yesterday when you were talking to the Storms. I went in to look at her this morning, since the funeral's supposed to be this afternoon, and that's when I noticed."

"Noticed what?"

"That her damn jewelry was gone, that's what," Ballinger said. "He called me and I came right down. There's no doubt about it. It's gone, all right."

"What's missing?" Rhodes said.

"Earrings again," Skelly said. "Wedding band. A couple of other rings, too. One of them had diamonds in it, or what looked like diamonds."

Rhodes looked at them. "Does her husband know?"

"Hell, no," Ballinger said. "Not yet. I guess we're going to have to tell him, though. It wouldn't be right just to bury her without letting him know."

Rhodes wondered if Ballinger had considered taking the chance.

"Besides," Skelly said, "he might notice."

"That's not the point," Ballinger said. "The point is, we're responsible. His wife was in our care, and we're responsible for what happens to her. Ballinger's has always given the best of care."

After that speech, Rhodes's faith was restored. Ballinger surely hadn't ever considered burying the woman without informing her husband of the loss. Rhodes wondered if sometimes he was too suspicious.

"What about the hired help?" he said.

"That might've been a pretty good idea when it was just Miss Storm," Skelly said. "But not now."

"Why not?"

"Because I'm pretty sure the jewelry was all on Mrs. West last night when I left," Skelly said. "And now it's gone. There wasn't anyone here last night except for old Don Spooner, who's kind of our night watchman, and he wasn't here when the other stuff was missing. So unless he's working as somebody's partner, it's not anybody who works here."

That didn't sound promising. "Who else would have access to the jewelry, then?" Rhodes said.

Ballinger looked glumly at his partner and shook his head. "That's the problem," he said. "Nobody does."

"Then where did it go?" Rhodes said.

"That's your job," Ballinger said. "You tell us."

"Are there any other bodies in there that I should know about?" Rhodes said.

"No," Skelly told him. "You're not going to try to say they're stealing from each other, are you?"

Rhodes didn't bother to answer. He didn't blame the two men for being upset.

"There's bound to be a logical answer," Ballinger said. "I just hope you can figure it out."

"I'll keep working on it," Rhodes said.

But he didn't have any very good ideas. To tell the truth, he didn't have any ideas at all. He left the two partners with their worries and went back to the jail. Ted Clayton was waiting for him when he got there.

Clayton was a big man, with broad shoulders and a deep chest. He had rugged features and a firm grip and reminded Rhodes of someone who might have played football in his younger days.

"Glad to meet you, Sheriff," Clayton said. "Sorry I was so hard to find yesterday, but I was working. I sell insurance, and there's never a day off if you have a prospect to visit."

Rhodes offered Clayton the chair by his desk and both men sat down.

"What kind of insurance do you sell?" Rhodes asked.

45

"I know what you're probably thinking," Clayton said. "The Dallas police have already been over some of this with me. You mind if I smoke?"

Rhodes didn't mind. He rummaged through the papers on his desk and came up with a glass ashtray surrounded by what looked like the world's smallest tractor tire. He had gotten it somewhere for nothing; it was an advertising gimmick.

Clayton brought a package of Marlboro Lights out of his shirt pocket and lit one with a navy blue Bic. "The thing is," he said, "I don't sell life insurance. If Sula, that's my wife, was anything, she was underinsured. I sell health insurance to small businesses, do a little workman's comp, things like that. The firm I work for sells life insurance, sure, but that's not my line."

He blew out a nervous stream of white smoke. "I know what the law usually thinks in a case like this, and like I said, the Dallas police have already talked to me. Right off they started asking me about insurance and things, especially after they found out that I sold it. But all I had on Sula was a small policy for ten thousand."

Rhodes watched him tap his cigarette on the edge of the tractor tire. "That's not very much for a man in the business," he said.

Clayton looked around the office. Hack was bent over the radio as if working on some part of it. Rhodes knew he was listening to every word, but Clayton seemed reassured.

"Look," Clayton said, "I wouldn't want my boss to hear me say this, but I don't really believe in life insurance. That's why I don't sell it. I figure it's a gamble, and win or lose, you lose. That's why I stick to health insurance. Now that's a necessity these days, what with the high cost of medical care, and it's something I can sell because I believe in it. Life insurance? Uh-uh."

Rhodes decided to change the subject before Clayton sold him a policy for major medical. "What happened between you and your wife?" he said.

Clayton tapped ash off the end of the cigarette, then looked

46

around the room again. Hack was still hunched over the radio.

"I don't know if I ought to say," Clayton said. "I still don't know if that's really her that you found at my place, do I?"

"No," Rhodes said. "You don't. But it seems like a very good possibility."

"Will I have to identify her?" Clayton said, a quaver in his voice.

Rhodes thought about the way Dr. White had described the condition of the body. "No," he said. "That probably won't be necessary. We'll have to request your wife's dental records, and we can make the identification that way. Do you know the name of her dentist?"

Clayton thought about it for a minute and then came up with the name. Rhodes had him write it on a piece of note paper.

"I don't know the address, though," Clayton said. "Just the name of the street."

"That ought to be enough," Rhodes said. "We can call him on the phone."

Clayton wrote the street name on the paper.

"What makes you so sure it's really my wife that you found?" Clayton said, crushing out his cigarette and lighting another one.

"She was in your house," Rhodes said. "She's been missing for three weeks. It seems to be a logical conclusion that it's her body."

Clayton sighed and leaned back in his chair. "I guess I ought to tell you about it, then," he said.

Rhodes didn't say anything, just looked at him encouragingly.

"I looked for her down here, you know," Clayton said. "First thing."

"No," Rhodes said. "I didn't know that." He wondered why the Dallas cops hadn't gotten in touch with him.

"I didn't tell anybody. It was something I didn't want to talk about. But I checked here before I went to the police. She wasn't here then."

"Maybe you just didn't look carefully enough," Rhodes said, thinking of where he and Ruth Grady had found the body.

"I just can't believe she's dead," Clayton said. "And that the house has been robbed. Do you think that whoever stole all my stuff is the one who killed her?"

"That's what I'm trying to find out," Rhodes said. "You say you searched for her here?"

"Yes."

Clayton looked as if he might have more to say on that subject, so Rhodes waited him out. One thing he had to say for working with Hack and Lawton—it had taught him patience.

Clayton took a long drag on his cigarette and sighed out the smoke. "I guess I might as well tell you about it," he said. "You'd find out anyway, and it just might be that the sonofabitch killed her."

Rhodes kept waiting. Sometimes that worked better than prodding.

"It's that fella Washburn," Clayton said. "The one that owns the house next to mine."

"What about him?"

"He's a smooth character," Clayton said. He crushed out his Marlboro and reached for another one. Then he thought better of it and shoved the pack back in his pocket. "He put the moves on Sula."

How do you mean?"

"She's a good-looking woman, Sheriff. Or she was, if that's really her over at your funeral parlor. Men were attracted to her, but she never paid them much attention, until that Washburn came along."

"What was so special about him?" Rhodes asked. He was trying to remember if he had talked to Washburn the day before and decided that he hadn't. Ruth must have been the one to interview him, and she must have done it after Rhodes had gone home. He made a mental note to check over Washburn's property inventory very carefully.

"I don't know that he was so special," Clayton was saying when Rhodes tuned back in to him. "He didn't look like

48

anything special to me, but then what do I know? I still don't know why women like that fella on *Moonlighting* so much. He doesn't look like much to me either."

Rhodes had seen *Moonlighting* only once, but he agreed with Clayton.

"Anyway," Clayton went on, "she liked him. He had a way of kidding around that she thought was real cute. And he was good looking, I guess, if you like his type."

"What type is that?"

"Sort of greasy and smiley," Clayton said. "I guess you know what people think of insurance salesmen. Well, he looks like what most people think an insurance salesman would look like. Gives the profession a bad name."

"Is he from around here?" Rhodes said.

"No. He just stays in that house on the weekends sometimes, like we did. I think he's from Houston."

That would make it harder for Rhodes to talk to him, especially if he had driven up only the day before to discuss the burglaries. It was a pretty good drive up to Clearview from Houston.

"So he and your wife were interested in one another," Rhodes said.

"I guess you could put it that way."

"And when she disappeared, you thought she might have come down here."

"I thought she might've been meeting him down here."

"Did she announce that she was leaving, or did she just sneak out in the middle of the night?"

Clayton fished out another Marlboro and lit it. "It wasn't exactly like that," he said.

"How was it, then?"

"We went to this party on New Year's Eve," Clayton said. "I had a little too much to drink. I admit that. I usually don't drink much at all, and when I do, I have a tendency to say too much. I get a little aggressive and say things I shouldn't say."

"What did you say that time?"

"She started it. She said something about me drinking too much and paying too much attention to some of the other

49

women at the party. So I said a few things about her and that Washburn. We got pretty loud about it. She slapped me and walked out. That was the last time I ever saw her.'' He looked down at the ashtray as if trying to make something of the pattern in the ashes.

"I guess some of the people at the party saw what happened," Rhodes said. "I'll need the names of the people who were there."

"Sure," Clayton said. "I understand. I can give you the names of the hosts." He wrote the names and address on the same paper with the name of his wife's dentist.

"Can you think of any reason Washburn might have for killing your wife?" Rhodes said.

"I've been thinking about it all the way down here," Clayton said. "I can just come up with one thing. I think that after the party, Sula drove down here in her own car and probably called Washburn. Then he came up from Houston and they got together at my place. I don't even want to think about what they might have done there.'' He shook his head. "But after that, I like to think she came to her senses. And that's when he killed her."

"For coming to her senses?" Rhodes didn't quite follow the logic.

"It wasn't that. Maybe she told him she'd made a mistake, that she wanted to come back to me. He probably couldn't take that. So he killed her."

Rhodes had heard worse motives, but then he had heard much better ones. He would reserve judgment until he had talked to Washburn, and maybe longer.

"You said something about her coming down here in her car," Rhodes said. "There was no car out there when we checked the place."

"That means they stole the car, too," Clayton said. "It must've been there."

Rhodes asked Clayton to provide him with a list of the property that was missing, including the car, which turned out to be a red 1986 Ford Escort.

"That's all I can think of," Clayton said when he finished

writing the list. "There's probably more, but I can't remember it right now."

"You'll need a complete listing for the insurance company, too," Rhodes told him. "I'm not going to ask you not to leave the county, but you'll have to keep yourself available through the Dallas police. I might need to talk to you again."

"I will," Clayton said. "Look. Are you sure that's my wife you found in the house?"

"I don't know who else it could be," Rhodes said. "We'll know for sure when we get the dental records and make a comparison. But I wouldn't hold out too much hope if I were you."

Clayton wiped a hand across his face and looked down at the floor.

"I'm sorry," Rhodes said. "I wish I could tell you differently, but it's just not likely that the body is anyone else."

"I understand," Clayton said. "I guess I was just hoping . . ."

Rhodes didn't know what else to say. There was no need to give the man false assurances. Who else could the body be?

Clayton shook his head. "This seems so senseless. Burglars, or that Washburn fella. How could it happen?"

"There's never a reason that makes sense to somebody on the outside," Rhodes said.

Clayton shook his head again. "I'll be where you can reach me. And I'll get in touch about the funeral arrangements if it turns out that Sula really is the one they . . . have."

"All right," Rhodes said. "I'll help out with that if I can."

"Thanks, Sheriff," Clayton said. He put out his hand, and Rhodes shook it. "I appreciate that."

Then he went outside into the cold.

Chapter 6

"WELL," RHODES SAID TO HACK. "What did you think?"

"About what?" Hack said. "I was busy with this here radio."

"I didn't notice any calls coming in."

"Maybe that's because there weren't any . . . Well, the fella seems all right to me. A little upset about his wife, but not too upset, if you know what I mean."

Rhodes knew what he meant. He had seen Lawrence Olivier's movie version of *Hamlet* one night on the PBS channel, and he remembered the line about protesting too much.

"You reckon there's any chance that ain't his wife?" Hack said.

"If you were a betting man—" Rhodes began.

"Which I ain't," Hack said.

"—it would be a good idea to get your money down on Sula Clayton being the one we found wrapped up in the tape," Rhodes finished.

"That's too bad," Hack said. "Course it'd be too bad if

it was anybody at all killed like that, not just that fella's wife. You think it happened like he said it did?''

''Who knows?'' Rhodes said. ''It might have. It might not. I'll find out.'' He hoped he sounded confident, although he didn't feel especially cocky about his chances.

The telephone rang.

Hack grabbed it. ''Sheriff's office.''

He listened for quite a while.

''Yes'm,'' he said. Then he said it again. ''Yes'm. Sheriff'll be right out.''

''He hung up. ''That was Miz McGee,'' he said. ''She said to tell you she saw that moving van again. It went down the road right in front of her house. I told her—''

''I heard you,'' Rhodes said. ''I'm on my way.''

''You want some backup?'' Hack said. ''You know, you've gotten yourself in some fixes before by goin' out without any.''

''I'll try to stay out of trouble,'' Rhodes said as he started through the door. Then he turned back. ''One thing. While I'm gone, have Ruth call that Officer Ferguson and see if Clayton happens to have a .38 registered to him.''

''It's her day off,'' Hack said.

''Then you call,'' Rhodes said.

''Talkin' to those big-city cops ain't in my job description,'' Hack said.

''A man's gotta do what a man's gotta do,'' Rhodes said as he went out.

The wind rocked Rhodes's car as he drove toward the lake. He hoped he could get there in time to catch up with the van. If he were lucky, he might even catch them in the act. He wanted to stop by Mrs. McGee's first, to ask her which way the van was headed, and he was curious to know how she had spotted it. Surely she hadn't been sitting out on her porch on a day like this one.

He turned down her drive in a swirl of leaves. The trees had been nearly bare before, and every leaf that had remained was now stripped off and blowing around the ground and into the air.

Mrs. McGee was not on her porch. Rhodes got out, the wind slamming his door for him, and climbed the steps to knock on the door.

She opened it and let him in quickly. "I declare," she said. "It's not a fit day to be out."

Rhodes agreed with her, though he was almost as comfortable in the biting wind as in the oppressive heat of her house. If anything, she had turned up the Dearborn heater even higher than the day before.

"I'm glad you got here so soon," Mrs. McGee said. She was still wrapped up in several sweaters, a scarf, and her knit cap. "I don't want those thieves to get away."

"They may already have gotten away," Rhodes said. "Which way were they traveling?"

"Let's see. I was standing at that window." Mrs. McGee indicated a window near the door. "I think my left would be the north and my right would be the south, so that means they were going toward the south. I think that would be right."

"Yes," Rhodes said. "That would be right. You're sure it was the same van?"

The old woman looked at him. "Of course I am. You think I can't tell one moving van from another one?"

"I didn't mean it that way," Rhodes said apologetically.

"That's all right," she said. "You just get after him."

Rhodes assured her that he would.

He went to his car, got in, and headed south after he left the drive. He didn't know much about the area, but he thought there were several houses in that direction that hadn't yet been broken into. He should have checked the patrol schedule before he left the jail to see if any of the deputies was out in the area, but it was right in the middle of the day and he doubted that anyone would be around. They really hadn't thought the burglaries were occurring in broad daylight.

Rhodes followed the narrow, winding gravel road, looking through the trees at the sparsely scattered houses as he drove. The road gradually moved away from the lakefront, and as the property became less desirable the houses were even more scattered.

54

Passing one house, he thought he caught a glimpse of green through the black tree branches. He knew it wasn't leaves, so he braked the car to a stop and backed up. He wasn't certain, but it appeared to him that there was indeed such a patch of color behind the corner of the house.

This house had the look of one long abandoned. The mailbox had fallen from the top of its post and was lying in a stand of tall dead weeds. Its lip hung open, and the whole box looked rusted. Rhodes couldn't see the name on the side because of the weeds. The house itself, what he could make out of it, was in bad need of a fresh coat of paint. The roof could have used a few shingles here and there, and one of the windows looked broken. Rhodes wondered just how long it had been since the owner checked on it.

He turned down the drive and when he came to the end pulled the car up crossways to block it. There was a little room on either side, but the trees there should be enough to stop anyone from trying to get by. He got out and drew his .38. He hoped he wouldn't have to use it, but you could never tell. Some burglars could get pretty feisty when threatened with the law.

He walked toward the front door of the house, listening for any noise from inside. He didn't hear a thing. He'd made too much noise of his own while driving up, and whoever was in there would have already had plenty of time to get quiet, hide, or prepare to escape.

The front door was not ajar, but there was a rusty screen door hanging from the bottom hinge and drooping across the doorway. Rhodes wasn't going to attempt an entrance by the front door, however. He walked down to the corner of the house and slipped around it suddenly, his pistol at the ready.

There was no one in sight, and no sign of the truck. If it was really behind the house, the vehicle was now completely hidden from sight. Maybe he had only imagined the patch of green.

Well, even if he had, he still had to check it out, though why anyone would want to burglarize this particular house he had no idea. There was certainly nothing to recommend it.

Or, he thought, maybe that was exactly what *did* recommend it—the very fact that it looked so long uninhabited. If the thieves had noticed the increased patrols, they would have been doubly careful about choosing their targets.

Rhodes had worked his way to the back corner of the house. He stepped around, his gun leveled. Then, something clubbed him in the wrist. The pistol went flying.

Rhodes's first thought was that he should have listened to Hack and brought some backup. He was forever getting himself into difficult situations, and there was no excuse for it. If any of his deputies had done the same thing, he would have spoken to them pretty harshly, but he always thought he could handle things.

He looked to his left and saw someone moving behind a dark window. Whoever it was had been waiting for him and had probably struck him with something like a baseball bat. He was lucky they had hit his wrist and not his head.

The pain in his wrist made itself felt just about then, or maybe everything was happening at the same time and he was just picking up the events separately. He doubled over and was almost sick to his stomach as he wondered vaguely if his wrist was broken.

He looked up when he heard the doors of a truck slam. It was the big green truck, all right. The engine turned over and caught. Then the truck was angling its front bumper in his direction.

He didn't have time to pick up the pistol. He started back the way he had come, moving considerably faster now.

The truck rumbled closer, right behind him.

He turned the corner of the house and headed for his car. There was a shotgun in the car, if he could get there in time. He didn't think he could make it, though, and swore that if he got out of this one he would put in some serious time on the Huffy Sunstreak. He held his injured arm across his stomach as he ran.

The truck plowed over a dead tree limb, and Rhodes heard the crack of it snapping in two. He didn't look back. The truck sounded as if it must be right behind him with the driver intent on running him down.

Rhodes made it to the car, but it was too late to get the shotgun. It was too late to do anything except find a place to hide. Unfortunately, there was no such place.

He dived for the car and landed across the hood, suppressing a groan as his wrist banged into the metal. He scrabbled for a hold with his good hand and tried to turn around. He knew he was safe now. He was sure the driver couldn't possibly get past the car.

He was wrong—or he was right. It all depended on how you looked at it.

There wasn't much room for the driver to get by the car, that much was obvious even to the driver, but it didn't seem to bother him any. He kept coming. When Rhodes saw what was about to happen, he groaned again, not from pain but from anticipation.

There was not room for the truck between the car and the trees, so the driver was going to make room in the only way he could—by moving the car. The hard way.

There was nothing at all that Rhodes could do. He didn't even have time to get a good grip on the windshield wipers.

The truck hit the front end of the county car with considerable force, throwing it aside and sending Rhodes flying through the air. He remembered thinking that the county commissioners were really going to be upset with him, and then he hit a tree.

Rhodes wasn't out long, but by the time he came to, the truck was long gone. He knew that he had muffed a chance to arrest the burglars, and he felt both foolish and guilty. His wrist hurt, his head hurt, and he didn't know where the .38 was.

He sat up and tried to assess the damage to his body. He couldn't even think about the damage to the car yet.

Luckily, he seemed relatively intact. There was going to be a knot on his head, his pants were torn, and there was a bad scratch across the back of his left hand. Add the right wrist to that inventory and you had the lot. It could have been worse.

It was time to find out if he could stand. . . . He could, so he walked over to the car.

The front fender was mashed into the tire, and he was going to have to pull it away. Otherwise, he would have to radio for help, and he really didn't want to do that. The bumper was mangled, the headlight broken, and the hood was sprung. He hoped the engine would start. There didn't seem to be any leakage from the radiator, so maybe the damage wasn't too extensive.

Before attempting anything to the car, he had to find his pistol. He walked slowly to the back of the house. The .38 was lying about where he had thought it would be, and it didn't look as if it had been run over by the truck. At least there was that to be thankful for.

He picked up the pistol and holstered it, thinking that he might as well have a look inside the house while he was back there. He was sure the back door would be open.

It was, and he went inside.

He must have caught the burglars right at the beginning of their work. Most of the furnishings seemed to be in place, not that they really merited stealing.

The kitchen looked as if it had been furnished with garage-sale items. There was a Formica-topped table, surrounded by four tubular metal chairs with red vinyl seats and bottoms. The vinyl was torn in several spots and gray stuffing peaked out. He guessed that the refrigerator was about a 1947 Crosley.

Rhodes looked in a couple of the other rooms, and the furniture there wasn't much better. This place must have been a real disappointment to the thieves. Rhodes secured the back door and went outside.

His wrist hurt, and he was beginning to feel some aches and pains throughout other parts of his body from the fall. He still hoped to be able to pull the fender away from the tire, however.

He got a good grip on the fender with his left hand and one that was not quite so sturdy with his right. He could feel the gritty dirt and grease that had accumulated underneath the car and was sorry that he didn't have anything to clean up with afterward. A lot of cops carried rubber gloves and antiseptics in their cars now, thanks to the almost universal fear of AIDS, but Rhodes hadn't yet begun to do so.

He gave a quick, hard pull, and the fender came away from the tire with a groan and a pop. He was pretty sure that if the car had been as sturdy as the ones he remembered from his childhood, he would never have been able to do the job. His grandfather had driven a 1941 Chevy with fenders that looked like they had been made from cast iron.

He pulled again and the fender moved a little more into line. It still looked terrible, and the bumper stuck out at a weird angle, but he thought he could drive back to town.

He wiped his hands on his pants, then regretted it. He was the one who would have to pay for cleaning and mending them, and he had left a long grease mark down one leg. He sighed. The one good thing that had resulted from the whole experience was that the exercise had made him forget just how cold it was.

He got in the car and started back to town, turning on the radio and hoping that it would either distract him or help him think. He picked up a country station playing a song by Randy Travis, one of the new country stars that gave Rhodes hope for the music. Travis actually sounded like a country singer and not someone trying out for a lounge job in Las Vegas. Along with Dwight Yoakum, George Straight, and a few others, Travis was making country worth listening to again. It was about time, in Rhodes's opinion. He had been listening to too many violins for too many years.

A song by John Conlee came on next. Rhodes thought Conlee's "Rose-Colored Glasses" was one of the great country songs, though the singer hadn't come up with one nearly so good in quite a while. This one was something about suburban living, and Rhodes mentally tuned it out and tried to concentrate on the burglary-in-progress that he had interrupted.

He could be almost certain now that there was an active gang of thieves operating in the area. He wondered just how many people had been in the truck. He really hadn't had time to look carefully, or even to catch a glimpse of the license plate. There had been a driver and someone in the seat beside him, but Rhodes hadn't seen either of them clearly.

It was also obvious that the thieves were nearing the end of their stay in Blacklin County, or at least in this section of it. The house where they had been spotted was hardly worth the effort. Rhodes was afraid that if he didn't stop them soon they would be long gone. In fact, his interruption of their efforts could have made them skittish, and they might decide to take off even sooner. It would now be clear to them that the law was breathing down their necks.

The car ran just fine all the way back to town, with the exception of a slight scraping noise when Rhodes turned a tight corner. The noise was bothersome, but Rhodes didn't think it meant much. Just the tire touching the fender, he told himself. Nothing to be concerned about. He preferred to believe that it wasn't scraping enough to damage the tire— or at least not enough to damage it too much.

"Good Lord," Hack said when Rhodes walked into the jail. "What happened to you?"

"It's a long story. You don't want to hear about it."

"I sure do," Hack said. "You look like you went a couple of rounds with a buzz saw. But I ain't got time to hear anything now. You get over to the funeral home. Clyde Ballinger just called. There's big trouble."

"What kind of trouble?"

Rhodes didn't feel like going over to the funeral home again. He wanted to go home and take a hot bath, eat some lunch, which he had forgotten to do again, and rest. At least his wrist was feeling better. He had forgotten about his vow to take a few minutes exercise on the stationary bike.

"He didn't say, but he sounded fairly desperate. There was a lot of noise in the background, like people yellin' and goin' on real loud. Not the kinda behavior you oughta have at a funeral parlor, if you ask me."

"Can't somebody else go?" Rhodes said.

"Maybe in an hour or so, but not right now. Ever'body on duty's too far off to get there. Except for you."

"And that's why they pay me the big money," Rhodes said. "Right?"

Hack didn't smirk. He wasn't capable of smirking. He did look very self-satisfied, however.

"That's right," he said. "You're the High Sheriff."

"Right," Rhodes said.

The hot bath would have to wait.

Chapter 7

RHODES COULD SEE about fifteen cars parked outside the funeral home as he approached. He drove to the rear and parked, entering through the back door. He could hear the ruckus Hack had mentioned. It sounded as if it might be coming from the direction of the Peace and Grace Room, so Rhodes headed that way.

There were twenty-five or thirty people in the room, and all of them were talking very loudly. The only quiet one, Rhodes thought, was the late Miss Storm, who still lay in her casket at the front of the room. The casket was open, and Rhodes could see Miss Storm's face staring placidly up at the ceiling. Everyone appeared to be dressed in his or her Sunday best, and Rhodes suspected that they were all there for Miss Storm's funeral service, which had apparently been interrupted for the shouting match.

Jack Storm and his wife were standing near the casket, talking to Clyde Ballinger or—more accurately—shouting at him. Storm's face was even redder than when Rhodes had seen him the day before, and that made his hair seem even whiter. He was standing toe to toe with Ballinger, wagging a thin finger in the funeral director's face. His mouth was open, and he was clearly expressing a strong opinion, which Rhodes could not hear because of all the other noise and milling around. Storm's wife was standing behind him, clearly giving him all her moral support, but her mouth was closed. She was apparently satisfied to let her husband do the talking.

Ballinger looked like a man who was trying his utmost to keep from exploding. As Storm continued to rant and wave his finger, Ballinger seemed to swell almost visibly. His chest expanded in his expensive suit, and even his face had begun to puff up.

Rhodes made his way through the crowd. He recognized a few of the people vaguely but hoped he wouldn't be called on to speak their names. They were people he had seen around the town and possibly even met, but with whom he wasn't well acquainted.

"Excuse me," he said, brushing by a portly man in a gray pin-stripe.

The man was saying something very loudly about the color of the rouge on Miss Storm's face. "Too red! They always get it too red here!"

He was talking to a tiny woman, no more than five feet tall. She was swathed in black and had on a black hat with a short black veil. Rhodes hadn't seen a woman in a hat in quite some time, but this woman was old enough to have worn the hat when it was first in style.

She didn't quite seem to understand the portly man's remarks. "Red! I'll have you know that Jane Storm was a member of the D.A.R. for thirty-five years! She was a better American than anybody in this whole room!"

She looked menacingly at the man from under the short veil, and his hands went up as if to protect himself from her.

Rhodes pressed on and into the middle of another argument, this one between two thin women wearing identical fur jackets. Or maybe the fur was not real. Rhodes never was sure these days. The women looked as much alike as their jackets, and he wondered if they were twins.

"They say Clyde Ballinger stole all her jewelry, every last

piece of it," the one on the right said. "Went right in her house and took it out of her dresser drawers. She always kept it in her dresser drawers, right under her—" She saw Rhodes and clamped her mouth shut in a thin red line.

"Clyde Ballinger never did such a thing," the other woman, the mirror image, said, ignoring Rhodes. "That Tom Skelly, he might, but Clyde never would."

As Rhodes moved by them, he gathered that the theft of the jewelry was the general topic of the conversation all over the room. He didn't have time to listen in, however, as the discussion near the casket seemed to be heating up. Storm had stopped waving his finger and was now tapping Ballinger in the chest with it, forcing the funeral director backward. Ballinger thrust up a hand, but Storm ignored it and continued to poke with his bony finger.

Rhodes thought that Ballinger might make a stand, but before he could, it was too late. The funeral director's calves struck the edge of the dais and he lost his balance. His arms flailed the air momentarily, but he was unable to save himself. Rhodes stretched out his arm as if to catch him, but the sheriff was still a good ten feet away. There was nothing he could do except watch in horrified fascination as Ballinger tumbled backward into the casket.

He didn't strike hard, but he hit the casket with enough force to dislodge it from its base. As Ballinger fell onto the dais, the casket began to wobble.

Rhodes pushed two or three people aside, trying to get there in time, but there was no way that he could. The casket's support had already begun to collapse, starting at its foot. The box turned sideways, dumping Miss Jane Storm's mortal remains right beside Clyde Ballinger, who lay there as if stunned.

He probably was, Rhodes thought, mentally if not physically.

If the crowd had been noisy before, they were virtually hysterical now. Rhodes could hear women sobbing, men yelling, and Mrs. Storm, Jack's wife, screaming. Rhodes couldn't understand what she was saying, which was probably just as well.

He reached the dais and stepped up, trying to think of some way to quiet the crowd. For some reason he drew his pistol, though he certainly was not even remotely considering firing it. The weight of it hurt his sore wrist, but he raised his hand anyway. Maybe it would give him the look of authority.

"My God," someone screamed. "He's got a gun!"

"Maniac! Maniac! Hit the floor!"

There was the clatter and crash of folding chairs being knocked this way and that and the thud of bodies falling to the carpeting. In the next instant, the only people Rhodes saw still standing were Tom Skelly, whom he had not noticed before, and the very short woman. Skelly was staring at him open-mouthed, but the woman was advancing on the dais, her hands balled into tiny fists.

"Go ahead and shoot, you cowardly sonofabitch," she said, stepping over the portly man, whose rear end stuck up in the air for a distance that looked half her height. "Shoot a poor defenseless little old lady, if you dare. But you better shoot straight, or I'll bust your teeth out."

Now that everyone—well, nearly everyone—was on the floor, the room was remarkably quiet.

"It's all right," Rhodes said in a loud voice. "I'm the sheriff. You people have been disturbing the peace, and I'm going to see that this matter is straightened out."

He looked to the back of the room. "Tom, I want you to clear everyone out of here except for Clyde and the Storms. We need to talk. Take them down to some other room and keep them quiet."

Skelly walked to the front, trying to maintain a dignified bearing. Under the circumstances, he did a pretty good job of it. When he got there, he began speaking in hushed but sonorous tones, directing everyone to rise and go down the hall to the right and gather in the Sweet Repose Room.

There was a great deal of shifting and mumbling, but gradually everyone got to his feet and began to leave the room, except for the tiny woman, who stood with her fists clenched as she glared at Rhodes.

"Go ahead and shoot me," she said. "But if you do, the members of the D.A.R. will tear you to pieces."

"No one is going to shoot anyone," Tom Skelly said soothingly. "Now come along, Miss Tremont."

Miss Tremont continued to glare at Rhodes for a moment, then turned to follow the others. Clyde Ballinger had managed to sit up and was holding his head in his hands when Jack Storm jumped for him. He got his hands on Ballinger's shoulders, forcing him backward and bumping his head on the casket. It made a hollow bonging noise.

Rhodes holstered his sidearm and bent down to separate them. "Stop it, you two," he said. "Let's have a little dignity here. It's your sister's funeral, after all, Mr. Storm."

Mrs. Storm let out a wail. "Yes! And just look at the poor thing!"

Rhodes had to admit that it wasn't a pretty sight. Miss Storm's hands and arms had been crossed on her breast, but now they had flopped out to her sides. Her carefully arranged hair was mussed, and a spray of flowers had somehow fallen across her legs.

"I want you and Jack to go sit down," Rhodes told Mrs. Storm. "As soon as Mr. Ballinger and I get this straightened up, I'll want to talk to you. Face the back of the room, why don't you."

Mrs. Storm reluctantly obeyed, and Rhodes gave Jack a little prod to help him on his way.

When they were seated, Rhodes knelt down and put his hand on Ballinger's shoulder. "You OK?" he asked.

Ballinger shook his head, more to clear it than to indicate a negative answer. "I think so." He looked around him. "What a mess. We'll never recover from this. Never."

"Sure you will," Rhodes told him. Privately, however, he had his doubts.

"Let's see if we can do something about the mess," Ballinger said, standing up.

Together they righted the sawhorses and rearranged the flowing material that served to cover them and act as a border around the casket. Then the two of them lifted the casket up and placed it on the sawhorses—no easy job for two men—

but Storm evidently hadn't bought one of the deluxe models. It was painful to Rhodes's wrist, but he didn't say anything. He didn't want to call attention to what they were doing.

Then they had to deal with the late Miss Storm, and there was just no dignified way to do it. Rhodes looked at the body and then at Ballinger. Ballinger looked at Rhodes.

"You're the expert," Rhodes said at last.

He glanced at Mr. and Mrs. Storm. They sat with their stiff backs turned on the scene.

"All right," Ballinger said, after a glance of his own in the same direction. "You grab her feet. I'll get the shoulders."

Rhodes moved the spray of flowers and pulled down Miss Storm's gown. Then he took hold of the ankles.

Ballinger took her shoulders and they lifted.

Miss Storm sagged a little in the middle. She was heavier than she looked, but they managed to get her up over the edge of the casket and inside it again.

Ballinger smoothed out the lining. "We'll never recover from this," he said again.

"What happened?" Rhodes asked.

"You want my side or their side?" Ballinger looked out at the Storms.

"Both, I guess," Rhodes said. "Let's go talk to them."

They stepped down from the dais and walked to where the Storms sat in rigid silence.

Rhodes pulled up two chairs.

"You don't look so good, Sheriff," Storm said. "Been in a fight?"

"You mean, besides this one?" Rhodes said.

"Wasn't a fight. Just a disagreement."

"That's what I want to hear about," Rhodes said. "The disagreement. Who would like to start?"

"It was all his fault," Storm said, with an accusatory look at Ballinger.

"I don't agree with that," Ballinger said.

"There's the problem, all right," Rhodes said. "Except that neither one of you is being very specific about just what you don't agree on."

"I'll try to explain, Sheriff," Ballinger said. "You see, yesterday after you left, I talked to Mr. Storm about the funeral. I told him that while I had a great deal of faith in you as a lawman, I didn't think that it would be possible even for you to solve the problem of who stole his sister's jewelry in one day. And I told him that the funeral really should go on as scheduled. When he left, I thought he understood."

Storm was turning redder, but he didn't say anything.

"Is that how it was?" Rhodes asked.

"Nope, it wasn't," Storm said. "The way it was, I thought he'd be sure we was satisfied before he done anything. But he didn't make sure. He just went right ahead with the funeral."

Ballinger couldn't restrain himself at that point. "But you showed up here for the funeral, right on time. All your friends were here. Why didn't you tell them it was all off if you thought it was?"

"Well, when you didn't call me one way or the other, I thought things had been made right," Storm said. "I thought you must've got some more jewelry and replaced Jane's, or something like that. It's your fault it's gone, that's for sure."

"I'm not admitting that," Ballinger said. "But even if I did, and even if I do have a legal responsibility, I only filed the insurance claim yesterday. I don't see how you could expect me to have made any replacements this soon."

"Thought you mighta done it out of your own pocket," Storm said. "That's what you oughta do, if you cared about your business."

"Now you listen to me," Ballinger said.

"I ain't gonna listen to you. It's all your fault." Storm was getting worked up again.

His wife plucked gently at the sleeve of his suit jacket. "Jack? Is Sis all right?"

It seemed to be the first that Storm had thought of his sister. He looked toward the dais. "She looks fine," he said. "Why don't you go check on her."

Mrs. Storm walked off in the direction of the casket.

"Look," Ballinger said. "I'm sorry we had this misunderstanding, but the only decent thing to do is to go on with the funeral. If we ever do recover the jewelry, we can decide then what to do with it. But right now, the important thing is to get this over with and go on with our lives.''

Storm got a stubborn look on his face, and his mouth set in a firm line. Rhodes thought it was time for him to break in.

''Clyde's right,'' he said. ''It's possible that the thieves are long gone from here, and your sister's jewelry with them. They might have melted it down and sold it to some gold dealer by now.''

Storm was horrified. ''They better not have,'' he said.

''It's a possibility that you should consider,'' Rhodes said. ''I think you should go on with the services. Everyone's here, everything's ready. It's the best thing to do.''

''Well . . . ,'' Storm said.

Ballinger saw that he had a chance. ''Believe me, Mr. Storm, the sheriff's right. Let's get it done.''

Storm gave in. ''All right,'' he said. ''But you better do what you can to get that jewelry back, Sheriff. It's important to me.''

''I will,'' Rhodes said.

''And you better get to checking on your insurance,'' Storm told Ballinger. ''I'm gonna have satisfaction, one way or the other.''

''Don't you worry,'' Ballinger told him. ''One way or the other, you'll get it.''

''I'll go get everyone,'' Rhodes said. He left the two men together and went to find Skelly and the others.

Skelly had everyone calmed down, and the minister who was to conduct the funeral was reading some soothing verses from the Psalms—maybe it was Proverbs. Rhodes wasn't sure. Rhodes explained the situation to Skelly and told him that he would be leaving.

''You sure you don't want to stay?'' Skelly said. ''This might get rowdy again.''

''I don't think so,'' Rhodes said. ''I need to get back to the jail.''

''Well, all right, if you think so.''

''I'm sure things will go just fine,'' Rhodes said. He

wanted to get out of there and have a Dr Pepper and maybe a bologna sandwich.

He stopped at the first place he came to, a GasQuick store, which had Dr Pepper in cans and some kind of packaged sandwiches that were full of various kinds of lunch meat and cheese. He preferred Dr Pepper in bottles, and he knew that the sandwich would taste like cardboard, but he didn't have time to go home.

While he was eating the sandwich, which tasted more like cellophane than cardboard, he thought of something that he should have thought of before. He knew that he would have to go back to the funeral home to check it out, but he decided to go to the jail first, to see if anything had come up. The funeral home could wait. After all, he didn't want to interrupt the services. They had already been interrupted enough.

Rhodes finished his Dr Pepper and sandwich, got in his car, and drove on over to the jail.

Chapter 8

SEVERAL THINGS HAD HAPPENED at the jail during Rhodes's absence. The most obvious evidence of this was that Hack and Lawton were waiting for him, both wearing looks of eager anticipation.

"He don't look so bad," Lawton said. "Not near as bad as I thought he would, from the way you talked."

"He looks better now," Hack said. "I bet he's cleaned up some."

"Never mind that," Rhodes said, cutting them off. "What about that call to Dallas?"

"I took care of it," Hack said. "Didn't take long. They prob'ly just looked in their computer."

"So what did you find out?"

"That Clayton doesn't own a gun of any kind, much less a .38. For whatever that's worth."

Rhodes knew it wasn't worth much. Guns were easy to come by in Texas—at garage sales, flea markets, and even burglaries like the ones that had been occurring at the lake. These weren't guns obtained through proper channels, and none would be registered to the current owner, if they were registered to any owner at all. Thinking about this, Rhodes got still another idea that would have to be checked out.

The thought slipped from his mind as he looked at Hack again. He could tell that the two men weren't through with him yet—not by a long shot.

"There's something else, isn't there?" Rhodes said.

"I guess you could say that," Lawton said. "I guess you could say there's something else. Ain't that right, Hack?"

"That's right," Hack said. "You could sure say there's something else."

Rhodes had forgotten whose turn it was to work him over, so he just waited.

"Miz Sterling called," Hack said at last, watching Rhodes's face.

Rhodes tried not to give anything away. "Oh," he said. Miss Sterling was a retired school teacher who lived on her retirement check and spent a great deal of her time calling the sheriff's office. "What did she want this time?"

"Says there's a peepin' tom in the neighborhood," Hack told him. "Says he's been lookin' at her for a long time now, and she wants something done about it."

"She's gettin' to be afraid of him, she says," Lawton put in. "Says that—"

Hack took over again. "Says that she thinks he might do something to her, and she wants you to get over there right away."

Why me? Rhodes thought, but he knew the answer. Everyone else was on patrol and too far away. Or that's what Hack would tell him, anyway.

"You might want to clean up a little first," Lawton said. "You still don't look as good as a sheriff oughta."

Rhodes ignored him and went out to the car.

Lawton was right behind him. "Hack and I been wonderin' how you got so banged up. Now I guess I know." He was looking at the car.

"I had an accident," Rhodes said. He got in the car.

As he drove away, he could see a look of pure joy on Lawton's face. He was really one up on Hack now, and

Rhodes knew he would have to tell them the whole story sooner or later.

On his way to the Sterling house, he reflected that one of the real problems with life was that you never had time to concentrate all your abilities on the really major problems. There were always the little, niggling things that came up and drained your energies.

Like right now. He had a murder on his hands. That was the major thing, but there were the burglaries, which were a major item in themselves and seemed to be tied in to the murder. If Clayton was telling the truth, then the murder suspects included the burglars and a man named Washburn, who Rhodes hadn't even met and who didn't live in the county. If Clayton wasn't telling the truth, and there was no particular reason to believe that he was, then he could be added to the list of suspects. That gave Rhodes two suspects living outside the county, along with the burglars. And then there were the thefts at Ballinger's. While not as big a problem as the burglaries, and certainly not as big as the murder, the thefts were definitely something to think about. Particularly if you were Clyde Ballinger.

But you couldn't devote yourself to thinking about those things all the time, especially if you'd done something foolish like wrecking one of the county cars and knew you'd be called to account for that. You couldn't even worry much about that, since you had to go see what was the matter with Mrs. Sterling.

Mrs. Sterling was glad to see Rhodes at her door. "Come on in, Sheriff," she said.

The front room was furnished like Rhodes expected of a retired teacher. There was a free-standing bookcase loaded with old textbooks with titles like *Adventures in Literature* and *The Literature of Britain*. The magazines on the coffee table included *National Geographic*, *U.S. News and World Report*, and *Mature Years*, and looked as if they had been lined up with a T square.

Mrs. Sterling herself was a formidable lady and reminded Rhodes of some of the teachers he had experienced as a child. At about five-eight and in the neighborhood of a hun-

73

dred and eighty pounds, she looked capable of eliciting a fearsome respect from her pupils. Her thick gray hair was piled up on her head in a roll and held in position with a number of huge plastic hairpins, the kind Rhodes's grandmother had used. He suspected that Mrs. Sterling had rarely had discipline problems in her classes.

"What seems to be the trouble, Mrs. Sterling?" Rhodes asked.

"He's watching me," she said.

"Who?" Rhodes said.

"Dan Rather."

"Dan Rather? The newsman?"

She nodded. "That's the one."

Rhodes didn't get it. "Are you sure it's not just someone who looks like him?"

"Oh, no," she said. "It's him. There's no doubt about that."

"How can you be so sure?"

Mrs. Sterling looked at Rhodes as if he were the one not making sense. "Why they say his name all the time. It's him, all right."

Uh . . . *who* says his name?"

"I don't know that." Mrs. Sterling sounded impatient. "What difference does that make?"

"Uh . . . none. None. You're sure he's watching?"

"Of course I'm sure. I wouldn't have called if I weren't sure. Have I ever called you when I wasn't sure?"

She has me there, Rhodes thought. She was always sure, even the time when she called about the man shooting electronic rays into her house. He had been a line repairman for the electric company.

"He watches me at the same time every day," Mrs. Sterling went on. "The same time."

Rhodes saw a remote-control device on the coffee table with the magazines. In one corner of the room there was a fairly new RCA ColorTrak set.

"At five-thirty?" Rhodes asked.

"Why, that's right. How did you know?"

"Just a hunch. He watches you?"

"Every move I make. He stares right at me, sitting there

in his pullover sweater like butter wouldn't melt in his mouth. But he's watching me. He can see me even when I'm in the kitchen.''

Rhodes stepped over to the TV set. From where he stood he could look through a connecting door and into the kitchen. He could see the porcelain sink and part of the counter top.

"I want it stopped," Mrs. Sterling said. "I don't want him watching me anymore."

"I'll tell you what, Mrs. Sterling," Rhodes said. "I don't think he'll watch you if you don't turn on your TV set at five-thirty."

"You're sure?"

"Pretty sure."

Mrs. Sterling looked relieved. Then she thought of something. "But how will I keep up with the news?"

Rhodes thought of a happy news team that spent so much time looking at one another they wouldn't bother Mrs. Sterling. He told her the channel. "Try watching that at six o'clock instead," he said.

"Well, if you think it will help," she said.

"If it doesn't, give me a call," he said, and immediately regretted it.

"Oh, I will, Sheriff. I will," she said, as she ushered him out the door.

He knew that wasn't an idle promise.

Before he went back to the jail, Rhodes drove by the funeral home. The service for Miss Storm was over, and the funeral party had moved on to the cemetery for the graveside ceremony. Tom Skelly hadn't gone with them, however, and Rhodes asked about events after the earlier altercation.

"It went all right," Skelly said. "There were no more outbursts, anyway."

"Good," Rhodes said. "I need to pick up something."

"What's that?"

"The tape off that body that came in yesterday. I want to get it fingerprinted."

"You want to fingerprint the tape?"

"Right. The sticky side of it especially."

75

They went into the room where Dr. White had worked. Sure enough, he had laid the tape out neatly—or as neatly as possible.

"I don't think you'll be getting any prints off the sticky side," Skelly said. "There's too much already stuck to it."

"I'll send it off to a forensic lab," Rhodes said. "It's something I have to try."

Rhodes had brought in several large evidence bags, and he tagged and bagged the tape while Skelly watched.

"There's one other thing," Rhodes said when he was finished.

"What's that?"

"You have a register for people to sign if they attend the funeral," Rhodes said. "Do they sign one if they come in for a viewing?"

"Sure," Skelly told him. "Lots of times people can't make it to the funeral or don't want to come, so they just view the body. Sometimes the family's here and sometimes not. We get everybody to sign in."

"I'd like to look at the Storm and West registers," Rhodes said.

"Sure," Skelly said. "Why?"

"I'm not sure. I can tell you more after I have a look."

"Why don't you go out to Clyde's office and wait. I'll bring the registers out there," Skelly said.

While Rhodes waited he thumbed through some of Ballinger's books. He was reading the first page of *The Diamond Bikini* when Skelly came in with the registers.

"That's a pretty funny book," Skelly said when he saw what Rhodes was reading. "It's about this guy named Uncle Sagamore, and he—"

"Not you, too," Rhodes said, putting the book back on the shelf.

Skelly looked sheepish, an expression Rhodes found incongruous on the funeral director's normally respectably solemn face. "Well, Clyde's always telling me how good they are. So I read one or two, and by golly, he's right. They are pretty good. Anyway, here's those registers you wanted to look at."

He handed Rhodes two leather-bound books, which Rhodes put on the desk and opened. He ran his finger down the list of names in the Storm book and then in the West book. He still wasn't sure what he was looking for, and whatever it was, he didn't find it.

"When you give these books to the Storms and the Wests," he told Skelly, "I want you to ask them to go over the lists very carefully, looking for the names of people they never heard of. If there are any, tell them to let me know as soon as possible."

"Why would someone they never heard of sign the registers?" Skelly asked.

"Maybe to steal their jewelry," Rhodes said. "You didn't happen to see the same people in both rooms at any time, did you?"

Skelly gave it some thought, but he couldn't come up with anything. "I don't think so," he said.

"Well, it was just a shot," Rhodes said. "Be sure to get those registers to the families and tell them to go over them. Today or tonight, if possible."

"I'll take care of it," Skelly said.

Rhodes thanked him and went back to the jail.

Hack was not in a particularly good mood, because Lawton had scooped him, so Rhodes had to calm things by relating the entire episode to them.

"Told you you shoulda had a backup," Hack said self-righteously. Rhodes could tell that saying it made him feel better.

"You were right," Rhodes said. "Either one of you know anything about the country down below the sound end of the lake?"

"There's some folks livin' in those parts that you don't want to mess with, I know that much," Hack said. "You ever done much travelin' back in there?"

"Not to speak of," Rhodes said.

"Just as well," Hack said, and Lawton nodded agreement. "There ain't no votes in that part of the county, or anything else but trouble."

"How do you mean?"

"There was a book out a long time ago, right after the War, seems like," Hack said.

Rhodes knew he meant World War II. For Hack, that was the War.

"*Tobacco Road,*" Hack said. "You ever read it?"

Rhodes admitted that he hadn't. "I saw the movie, though."

"Me, too," Hack said. "These people I'm talkin' about—the ones down below the lake—well, they live like that. In shacks like that, or worse."

"I've seen 'em," Lawton said. "He's right about it."

Rhodes had seen them, too, now that he thought about it.

"There's a whole nest of 'em back in there," Hack went on. "They don't live that way because it's the best they can do. They live that way because they like it. I guess you could say they're the closest thing to outlaws we got in this day and age."

Rhodes was thinking that he should have looked there for the truck in the first place, but it was easy to forget the existence of places like that, as long as there was no trouble. The people Hack had described weren't outlaws in the sense that they were constantly in trouble with the law—only in the sense that they had chosen to live outside the regular stream of life, making their own rules and regulations. They probably had never paid taxes, never voted, never done any of the usual little things most citizens took for granted. Rhodes wouldn't have been surprised if they owned one or two license plates among them, which they would change from truck to truck or car to car whenever they took a trip into town.

"I guess I should go down there and look around," Rhodes said.

"I wouldn't go today," Hack said. "It's gettin' too late, and after dark you could come into some real trouble." He looked at Rhodes's torn pants and the scratch on the back of his hand. "Not that you don't do a pretty good job of that in the broad daylight."

"I'll wait," Rhodes said. "And when I go, I won't go alone."

"They won't bother you, 'less you bother them," Lawton said. "What've you got in mind?"

"I'm just going to look for the truck," Rhodes said. "I guess it would be too much to hope for that the name of the truck buyer would be the name of somebody living back down there."

"If some of them bought a truck, you can bet their name won't be on the list. Or on the title, either," Hack said. "And if they know you saw the truck, which they surely do, you won't find it anywhere around. You can count on that."

"It's too good a truck to get rid of completely, though," Rhodes said. "They might just try to hide it."

"They might be better at hidin' than you are at findin', though," Lawton said. "When they see that county car, that truck'll be long gone."

Lawton was right, Rhodes knew. One of the reasons there was never any trouble from that area of the county was that the people there took care of it themselves and never exposed it to the view of the rest of the world. It was entirely possible that anyone causing trouble there would simply disappear from sight, never to be seen again. It was suddenly quite plausible that the burglars could also be killers.

With that thought in mind, Rhodes ended the conversation. He spent the rest of the afternoon working on a report about the wrecked car, wondering how he could make it look reasonable to the commissioners.

Chapter 9

"So," Ivy said. "When do you think we should get married?"

"Uh," Rhodes said. It was the best he could do under the circumstances. He found himself wondering why she had started her sentence with the word *so*. He had heard lots of people on TV begin sentences that way, but he had never heard anyone in Texas do it. He wondered if they had been watching too much TV. Then he realized that his mind was seeking refuge in irrelevancy and tried to drag it back to the subject at hand. Marriage. How had that come up?

They were at his house again, watching *The Hired Gun*, in which Rory Calhoun was playing a gunfighter hired to track down Anne Francis. Rhodes had always liked Calhoun. He had even read a book Calhoun had written, a Western novel published by some paperback company in California. He wondered if Calhoun was still writing books. It had been quite a while since he read that one, and he couldn't recall the name of it. Probably Ballinger would know. He might even have a copy. Rhodes would have to ask him about it the next time he saw him.

Chuck Connors was in the movie, too. Rhodes had seen him recently in a TV show, playing a werewolf. It wasn't a very good show, but—

Ivy poked her fingers into Rhodes's ribs.

"When?" she said.

It wasn't that the subject hadn't entered his mind. He'd thought about it a lot. Or he had thought around the edges of it. He somehow just couldn't quite bring himself to think *about* it. Even when he had given her the ring, he hadn't set a date, not even in his mind.

Ivy jabbed him again.

"Last chance," she said.

"February twenty-seventh," he said. It just popped out. Well, that wasn't exactly true. For a horrible moment there he had almost said February twenty-ninth. It would have been just a joke, but there really was a February twenty-ninth coming up, and it was possible that Ivy wouldn't have appreciated the joke. At least he thought it would have been a joke. Maybe he was serious, but February twenty-seventh was over a month away. A lot could happen in a month.

"That sounds fine," Ivy said. "I didn't mean to be pushy."

"It's all right," Rhodes said.

He didn't think she was pushy. He just thought that he was wishy-washy. He knew he wanted to marry her; he just couldn't make himself say the words. Now he didn't have to worry about it.

"You have to admit it's about time," Ivy said.

They weren't watching the movie anymore, but Rhodes didn't mind. In fact, he felt better than he had in a long time. He knew that they were doing the right thing, and he wondered why he had put it off for so long. He wondered if he would have ever made the move if Ivy hadn't poked him in the ribs. Probably not, he decided. It was a good thing that Ivy wasn't shy about things like that. It wasn't that she was aggressive. Just sensible.

"I'll have to write my daughter," he said.

"I don't think she'll be too surprised," Ivy said. She was probably right.

81

"I'll have to tell Hack and Lawton, too." Preferably while they were both in the room at the same time, he thought. "And the deputies."

Aside from that, there weren't many people he should inform. He didn't have much of a social life, and never had. There was too much to do on the job, and whenever he really tried to get away, he got called back almost immediately. His free time was spent mostly at home, watching the old movies he enjoyed so much, within easy reach of the telephone when it rang. A great deal of that time had once been spent with Clare, his first wife, and now he was sharing it with Ivy. It looked as if he would be sharing even more of it with her in the future."

"We can get the judge to marry us," Ivy said. "I don't think we need any kind of formal service, do you?"

Rhodes didn't. "I have to see the judge tomorrow anyway," he said. The county judge presided over the meetings of the county commissioners, and Rhodes would have to tell him about the wrecked car.

Ivy hadn't heard the story of the car, so Rhodes told her.

"I'd hate for you to get killed before the wedding," she said. "Can't you be a little bit more careful?"

"I am careful," he said. "It seems like these things just keep happening to me." One of the reasons he hadn't asked Ivy to set a date, he told himself, was that his job was extremely dangerous. He didn't want to leave her a widow a second time.

"What about the truck that hit you?" she asked. "Did you try to follow it?"

"No. By the time I picked myself up and got going, it was too late."

He decided it might be best not to mention that he had been knocked unconscious. He hadn't told that part of the story to Hack or Lawton either. They would have insisted that he go to the emergency room and get checked out, and Ivy would have felt the same way. Rhodes didn't want anyone taking care of him.

"But you saw which way they went?"

"Yes," he said, which wasn't exactly true, but he was

virtually certain they had gone south, to the area he had discussed with Hack and Lawton. He told her about that.

"And no doubt you're planning to go in there and see if you can find the truck."

"Well . . . yes," he said.

"Are you sure that's a good idea?"

It was the best idea he had. He wasn't going to send anyone else, that was for sure. "Maybe not," he said. "But it's all I can come up with."

"Be careful, then," she said.

That was all she said, and he was grateful. He wouldn't have known how to handle it if she had told him not to go or to send a deputy. He had been afraid that the setting of an actual date might have made her overly protective, but he should have known better. She wasn't going to change.

"I'll be careful," he said.

"Good. Now, are we going to live in your house or my house?"

The norther had blown through by the next day. The sun was shining, the sky entirely blue, and the temperature in the low thirties. It was a beautiful day, but still cold.

Rhodes dressed in a pair of faded jeans, a brown-and-blue flannel shirt, and an old down jacket that at sometime in the past had developed a large rip on the right side and had never been repaired.

He went out into the yard and called Speedo, who poked his nose out of his barrel tentatively then raced around the yard, barking. Rhodes broke the ice that skimmed the top of the water bowl and poured some Old Roy in the food dish. Speedo wolfed down the food and lapped the water noisily.

"How would you like to do a little undercover work?" Rhodes said.

Speedo raised his head and looked at Rhodes questioningly.

"It might be dangerous," Rhodes said.

Speedo wagged his tail as if to say he didn't care.

"All right, then," Rhodes said. "Let's go." He walked over to the pickup and let down the tailgate.

Speedo jumped in, his toenails clicking on the metal as he tried to get a grip.

"We'll get started on our secret mission in a little while," Rhodes said. "First, we have to see the judge."

When they got to the courthouse, Rhodes told Speedo to stay in the pickup. Speedo didn't appear thrilled by the suggestion, but he didn't try to jump out.

Rhodes walked down the broad marble hall, climbed the wide stairs to the second floor, and went to the judge's chambers. It was still early, barely eight o'clock, but he had a feeling that Jack Parry would already be in.

Rhodes tapped on the door.

"Come on in," a voice called.

Jack Parry was sitting behind the large wooden desk, already smoking a big cigar. Rhodes didn't mind. He liked the smell of cigars. Parry had on a dark blue three-piece suit and was studying a piece of paper. He looked as if he had been at work for hours already. When elected to his office, he had worn a full beard, but he had shaved it recently and looked several years younger, though the bareness of his face emphasized the baldness of his head.

Rhodes ran his hand through his hair, an unconscious gesture.

Parry put down the paper. "Well, Sheriff, how's it going?"

"All right, I guess," Rhodes said.

"I know we don't have a county dress code, but aren't you dressed a little casually for a sheriff?" The cigar danced as Parry talked.

"I've got a little undercover work to do," Rhodes said.

"I see. Say, did you hear the one about the Aggie and the Longhorn that were rooming together for the summer?"

"I don't think so," Rhodes said.

"They made a bet about how many women they could get over the weekend. Well, the Aggie went out to a singles bar and got started. Finally picked one up and got her to take him home. Then went back to the room and put a mark on the wall. Found him another one, took a little longer this time. He was already getting tired, you see."

Rhodes nodded.

"Well, he did his do, went back to the room, made another mark on the wall. By now, he's really tired, but he goes out again. Finally finds a third one, gets her to bed, goes home, puts a mark on the wall. He can barely get his pen up to make the mark. By that time, it's too late to go back out. The weekend's nearly over. So the Aggie just collapses on the bed, just as the Longhorn comes bounding in. The Longhorn sees the three marks on the wall and just stops cold. His mouth falls open. He can't believe it. 'Damn!' he says. 'A hundred and eleven! Beat me by two!' "

The judge roared with laughter. Rhodes, who had attended neither the University of Texas nor Texas A&M, was more restrained. He understood the rivalry between the two schools, but he didn't think the joke was that funny.

"Well, you didn't come here just to hear my jokes," Parry said. "And this early, you must have something pretty serious on your mind."

Rhodes told him about the car.

"The commissioners won't be too happy with that little item," Parry said, removing his cigar and studying the tip.

"I didn't think they would," Rhodes said. "It was in the line of duty. Unavoidable. I wasn't even in the car."

"You'll get to tell it to them," Parry said. "They might think twice about that computer you've been wanting, though."

"Insurance will cover the car," Rhodes said.

"You're probably right. Nothing to worry about, unless the rates go up too much. You didn't give yourself a ticket, did you?"

They laughed together.

Parry put his cigar in an ashtray shaped like a boot. "Those the guys you're planning to drop in on in your disguise?"

"Those are the guys."

"I've never heard a good word about them," Parry said.

"Me neither," Rhodes said. "I'll be careful."

"You do that. I'd hate to lose a good sheriff." Parry picked up the cigar and stuck it back in his mouth, even though it was no longer burning. "And be sure you've got good insurance on that truck."

"There's one other thing," Rhodes said.

"What's that?"

"I want you to marry me and Ivy Daniel."

"Well, well. I was wondering when that was going to take place. Anytime soon?"

"February twenty-seventh," Rhodes said.

"I'll put it on my calender," Parry said, riffling through the pages of his desk calendar, which lay open on his desk. "What time of day?"

Rhodes hadn't thought about that. "I don't know. How about two o'clock?"

"Fine by me," the judge said. He made a note on the calendar. "Is this a secret or can I tell people?"

"Who'd want to know?"

"You'd be surprised," Parry said. "There's even a pool up in the courthouse here. I'll have to check to see what day I got."

Rhodes was surprised to hear there were that many people taking an interest in his personal life. He'd thought that hardly anyone even knew he was going out with Ivy.

"I'm shocked," he said, "to discover that gambling is going on here."

"Wait a minute, I know that one," Parry said. "Don't tell me. Uh, it's from *Casablanca*, right? Peter Lorre?"

"Claude Rains," Rhodes said.

"I was close, anyway," Parry said.

"Close doesn't count," Rhodes said.

"I know, I know. Except in horseshoes and hand grenades. See you at the commissioners' meeting—and on February twenty-seventh."

"I'll be there," Rhodes said.

There was nothing of great interest happening at the jail. Rhodes told Hack to have Ruth Grady get in touch with Washburn and ask him to come in.

"She doesn't have to tell him that he's a suspect in a murder investigation," he said, "but if he gives her any trouble about traveling up here, she can get tough."

"I'll tell her," Hack said.

"Where's Lawton?"

"Checkin' the cells. We got us a couple of Sunday drunks up there that need watchin'."

"Get him down here."

"What's goin' on?" Hack said.

"Nothing. Just call him."

Hack went to the door that connected the office area with the jail proper and called Lawton.

"All right," a voice replied. "I'm comin'."

In a minute or two Lawton entered the office. "What's the trouble?" he said.

"No trouble," Rhodes told him. "I just wanted to say something to you two."

"What?" Hack said.

"Ivy and I are getting married."

The two old men looked at each other, then back at Rhodes.

"When?" they said, almost in the same breath.

"In February."

"When in February?" Hack said.

"The twenty-seventh."

Hack looked at Lawton. "When did you have?"

"I can't remember," he said, "but I think it was in March anyway."

"Better'n me," Hack said. "I got April. There's a lot took June, though. We came closer than they did."

"What are you two talking about?" Rhodes said, though he thought he knew.

"The pool," Hack said. "There's a pool over at the court-house about when you and Ivy're gonna get hitched."

"How much did it cost you to get in this pool?" Rhodes said.

"Just five bucks," Lawton said. "I hear there's nearly forty people in on it. That'd be about two hunnerd bucks for the big winner." He looked at Hack. "I wonder if anybody's got February twenty-seventh?"

87

Hack shook his head. "I don't know. If nobody does, whoever got closest is the winner. That's the way it was set up."

"I can't believe this," Rhodes said.

"I don't see why not," Hack said. "Ever'body gets interested in a thing like this. You know how it is in a little town. If the sheriff gets married, it's a big deal."

Rhodes still couldn't believe it.

"I wonder how Miz Wilkie is gonna take this?" Hack said.

Mrs. Wilkie'd had Rhodes in her sights for a long time. She didn't take it too well when he began seeing Ivy, and she still hadn't given up her hopes entirely.

"Maybe nobody'll tell her," Lawton said.

"I don't know about that," Hack said. "She's into ever'thing that goes on around here. She'll find out, sure as shootin'."

"Don't worry about it," Rhodes said. He hoped he wouldn't have to deal with Mrs. Wilkie again. She was a hard woman to ignore. "There's something else I have to tell you."

"You gonna tell us why you're dressed like a duck hunter?" Hack said.

"That's exactly right," Rhodes said. "I'm taking your advice and not going down below the lake in the county car. I thought I'd go like this and drive my pickup. That way I might have a chance to see something or talk to someone."

"Surely you ain't about to go down there all by yourself," Hack said. "You got to have a backup."

"I've got Speedo with me," Rhodes said.

Hack snorted.

"I was only kidding," Rhodes said. "He's part of the disguise. I want you to tell Ruth Grady to stand by to get me out of any trouble I get into. Send her down to the lake and tell her to give me two hours." He glanced at his watch. "If I don't meet her at Mrs. McGee's house by eleven-thirty, tell her to head south and look for me."

"There's won't be nothin' left of you for her to find,"

Hack predicted. "They'll have you buried in a garbage dump 'fore she ever gets there."

"I'll try to hang on," Rhodes said.

"Some people'll do anything to keep from gettin' married," Lawton said.

"Not me," Rhodes said. "I'm looking forward to it."

Speedo was still in the pickup bed, but Rhodes could tell that the dog wanted to get out and get into action, even if the only action he got into was running around the truck. Rhodes rubbed his head. "It won't be long now," he said.

The drive to the lake was pleasant. The weather had warmed up into the forties, and the country station Rhodes was tuned in to had been playing songs that he liked to hear, George Jones's "He Stopped Loving Her Today," which Rhodes thought was maybe the perfect country song, though he had to admit it didn't mention one of the topics Steve Goodman once said were necessary for the perfect country song: prison, trains, mamas, and trucks.

Speedo enjoyed the ride, too. He barked at the passing cars, his ears flapping in the frigid breeze, his nose pointed into the wind. It wasn't often that he got to go for a long ride. Rhodes told himself that he should take the dog out more often.

Things became less pleasant as they headed south past the lake. The county commissioners didn't get any votes from down in there, and the roads were not kept up nearly as well as the ones near the better property. There were deep ruts in some places, and Rhodes had to keep a firm grip on the wheel. The ditches on the roadside rarely got cleaned, and they were choked with brush, not to mention aluminum beer cans. Now and then there were wide, washed-out places that someone had used for a trash dump, filled with plastic garbage bags, grocery sacks, cans, and assorted papers. There was no one around to enforce the littering laws.

Rhodes drove until he came to a house. It was set back off the road, but not far. There was no hint of grass in the front yard, not because of the winter cold, but because the dirt was too hard-packed to allow grass to grow. The yard was even more rutted than the road from the cars that had been driven into it and parked.

The house itself looked as if it had been put together by a drunk man, and maybe it had. It was a frame house up on wooden blocks that had probably been made from cedar stumps. Part of one side was painted blue, and the rest of it was painted white. There was no clear line where one color left off and the other began. The windows appeared to have no glass in them, but it was hard to tell because they were all covered with quarter-inch plywood. There were a couple of pitiful cedar trees in the yard, and an old Ford, about a '67, was parked beside the house. On the small front porch there was a gigantic red-and-green candle, probably a left-over Christmas decoration. A black stovepipe poked through a roof that was mostly tarpaper minus the shingles, but there was no smoke coming from the pipe.

Rhodes drove by slowly, but saw no sign of life. There was no place to hide a large green truck, either, so he drove on down the road. He passed several similar houses in the next couple of miles, but there was nothing particularly suspicious about them. Then he saw the one with the barn.

Chapter 10

IT WASN'T MUCH of a barn. It looked as if it had been built in a hurry and then abandoned for thirty or forty years. The tin roof was only partially in place, and Rhodes could see rusty segments of corrugated tin lying in the trees beyond. Those pieces of tin could have been blown off by Saturday's norther, or they could have been blown off years before. There was no way to tell.

The house wasn't in much better shape than the barn, but at least some of the windows had glass in them. There was no candle on the porch, but a hand-lettered sign nailed to a pecan tree said "BeWAR oF THe DOg." Rhodes didn't see the dog. He drove into the yard and parked beside a battered Dodge pickup that had once been black. It was now rusted and scraped so badly it had almost no color at all.

When Rhodes got out of his own pickup, he turned to Speedo. "You stay put, you hear?"

Speedo's answer was a low growl. Rhodes looked around, but still didn't see the dog the sign warned of. Then he heard a rumbling noise from underneath the porch. He peered in, but it was too dark to see anything, though he thought he caught sight of two big eyes. He decided not to walk up and knock on the door.

"Hello," he called. "Anybody home?"

There was no answer, but he waited patiently. If anyone was in there, normal curiosity would get the better of them sooner or later. It didn't matter where you lived. If there was a stranger parked in your front yard, you would eventually go out to see what he wanted.

No one came. Where was everyone today? Rhodes wondered. He continued to stand, leaning on his pickup, for nearly five minutes.

All right, he thought. If no one's here, I'll just have a look in that barn. He walked to the back of the truck and let down the tailgate. Speedo jumped down, and they walked together toward the dilapidated barn. Speedo's neck hair was ruffled and he looked back over his shoulder at the house several times. Rhodes hoped that whatever was under there would stay put.

The rough ground made for hard walking. Rhodes had to be careful not to step in a rut or on a clod and turn an ankle. Speedo followed him closely, never getting more than a foot away.

When they got to the barn, Rhodes saw that it was sturdier than it had looked from the road. Although it did seem almost to lean at an angle, the boards were tight and in fact had been repaired in several places with relatively new one-by-fours.

There was no door in the side of the barn that faced the road, so Rhodes and Speedo walked around to the other side, where there was a large open area, covered only by the remains of the tin roof. A feed trough made of wood was mostly rotted away.

The rest of the barn was taken up by a storage room that looked to be about ten by fifteen feet. The room had probably once been used to store hay and store-bought feed, but from the looks of the trough there hadn't been any feed to keep in there in years.

So why did the room have a practically new door, with bright hinges and a new brass padlock on it?

There was no legal reason for Rhodes to open the door. There was no truck here, and no way there could be a truck in that room. He had no probable cause to open the door. No judge in the world would give him a search warrant to open it. Still, it was clearly suspicious. He walked closer, with Speedo trotting at his heels, to see if there was a way he could peer in between a crack in the boards.

There was a deep-throated growl at his back, and he and Speedo turned together to find themselves facing a supremely self-confident pit bull.

"I should have known that if there was anything in this place, they wouldn't have left it without a guard," Rhodes said to Speedo.

The words were meant as an apology, but Speedo didn't hear them. He was concentrating on the other dog. Rhodes had come across Speedo on another case and had taken him home when his owner was killed. Speedo had been no great shakes as a watchdog. He was fairly big, obviously part collie, along with several other strains, all of them obscure, but Rhodes wasn't sure what kind of fighter he'd be.

On the other hand, Rhodes was pretty sure what kind of fighter the pit bull would be. Whoever lived here wouldn't have it around if it were a pussycat. It had been lying in wait underneath the house. When they went too far in their trespassing it came out after them.

Rhodes wished he had brought his pistol with him, but he had left it off. It wasn't even in the pickup. He'd decided that his only weapon was diplomacy.

"Good boy," he said.

The bull growled and advanced a step. Rhodes didn't think diplomacy was going to work. Besides that, Speedo was now definitely taking up a defensive posture, but from behind Rhodes.

Rhodes looked around. There was nowhere to run. He couldn't get into the storage room, and there was nowhere else to go. Barns were supposed to have lofts, but this one didn't. He had seen many an old movie where a man involved in a barn fight would grab a handy pitchfork and go after his attacker with a vengeance. Here, there were no pitchforks in sight.

Rhodes took a tentative step backward, and nearly stepped on Speedo. The bulldog took a step forward, keeping the distance between them the same. The hair along his backbone was beginning to stand up, and his teeth were bared.

Rhodes was just as glad Speedo wasn't trying to defend them. The bulldog would have ripped him to shreds. Speedo wasn't a small dog, but he was clearly no match for the pit bull.

There was no loft and no pitchfork, but there might be something Rhodes could throw. He looked around, but didn't see a thing.

Rhodes heard a car on the road and hoped it would go on by. The only thing worse than being trapped here by the dog would be to have the dog's owner show up and find him.

The car stopped in the yard, and Rhodes heard two doors slam. Just his luck. When things started going bad, they never seemed to improve. He sneaked a look at his watch. Not quite eleven o'clock. Ruth Grady wouldn't even begin to look for him for another thirty minutes.

"Samson," a deep masculine voice called from the front of the house. "Samson. . . . Now where in the hell is that sumbitch? If he's off chasin' rabbits again, I swear I'm gonna skin his ass. . . . Samson!"

The third time was the charm. The pit bull barked, lowered his head, and charged Rhodes.

Rhodes froze momentarily as all the stories about pit bulls that he had ever seen on the six o'clock news flashed through his head. Pit bull mangles mailman. Pit bull mauls toddler. He knew that pit bull owners hated those stories and insisted they were merely isolated examples of vicious behavior and similar examples could be found about any breed if you looked—but the fact remained that it wasn't just any breed that was charging him at that moment.

Speedo began to bark frenziedly but stayed behind Rhodes's legs, perhaps under the illusion that he was protected there.

About three feet from Rhodes the dog jumped. It wasn't

built for jumping, and the absurd sight unfroze Rhodes. He reached out and grabbed at the dog. He didn't know why he did that. It just seemed like the thing to do.

He surprised himself by getting a handful of fur and skin, and let the dog's momentum carry him into a turn. He could feel the dog's teeth snapping at him. Without thinking too much about it he let go of his hold, trying to put a little wrist into his throw. The dog sailed away and hit the door of the storehouse with a solid and very satisfactory thud.

Unfortunately, the dog was only stunned. Rhodes could hear his feet scrabbling at the hard ground almost as soon as he hit. Rhodes was already off and running, Speedo at his heels, barking wildly. Rhodes came up short at the rotting feed trough, bent down, and grabbed at one of the wooden legs, which was made from a four-by-four. He straightened and turned just as Speedo skidded by him, his claws seeking a grip on the packed earth.

Rhodes had never been much of a baseball player, but he put his arms into the swing he made at the charging pit bull, who, not having learned a thing from his previous attempt, once more launched himself into an awkward dive.

Rhodes connected solidly with the side of the dog's head, knocking him aside and down but not far, because the dog was too big and heavy. This time the bull lay still, but his sides heaved. He was still breathing, though not as heavily as Rhodes. Speedo trotted over to the bull and stood over him, barking.

Rhodes had to smile. "Great job," he said.

"That dog damn well better be all right, mister," a deep voice said. "If he ain't, I'm gonna kill you and your dog, too."

The man who had spoken was as big as a bear, had a three-day beard that somehow did not look nearly as fashionable as it did on a lot of TV stars, and wore heavy laced boots. He was also wearing about three flannel shirts, one over the other, with the lower layers revealed at the neck and wrists. Also revealed was the Saturday Night Special he held in his right hand, a .22-caliber pistol probably made in Bulgaria or some equally unlikely place, but no less deadly for all that.

There were some people who weren't afraid of a .22. Rhodes had talked to them. Their general theory was that a .22 had no stopping power and that a man with five or six .22 bullets in him could keep right on going and still have the strength to overwhelm his assailant—which proved that they really had no idea what they were talking about. Those little bullets could tumble around inside you and hit any number of vital organs before they ran out of steam. Just one of them, if it moved around in there enough, could do as much damage as a .357.

The man with the pistol spit a brown stream of snuff onto the dirt and wiped the back of his left hand across his mouth. That was when Rhodes heaved the four-by-four at him.

The man threw up his hands to block the board. The pistol went off as his finger reflexively pulled the trigger, and Rhodes and Speedo jumped him at the same time.

Why his dog had gotten so brave all of a sudden, Rhodes didn't know, but to tell the truth, Speedo was more of a hindrance than a help, barking and slobbering as Rhodes tried to get a grip on the man's gun arm.

The man twisted under Rhodes and tried to hit him with the pistol. Rhodes moved his head aside, and Speedo got a grip on the man's wrist. The man howled, or tried to howl. It sounded more as if he might be strangling on his snuff.

Rhodes grabbed the pistol and struggled into a sitting position on the man's chest. Holding the gun in his left hand, he clipped the man on the point of the chin with his right. His teeth clicked together and he quit howling. Speedo released the man's wrist. Rhodes stood up, glad to get away from the man, who, he had just noticed, smelled worse than Speedo's breath.

The pit bull was beginning to stir, but now that he actually had a pistol Rhodes had no desire to shoot the dog. He walked over to the trough, laid the pistol in it, and grabbed hold. He dragged it over to the bull, removed the pistol, and toppled the trough over on the dog.

Let him bite the inside of the trough for a while, Rhodes thought. It might be good for his teeth.

"Looks like you have everything under control," Ruth Grady said.

Rhodes looked around. Ruth was there, holding her pistol pointed at another man, this one much smaller than the one on the ground, but just as mean-looking. He was dressed in a similar fashion and wearing a yellow gimme cap on which the initials a.p.f. were placed in a horizontal row beside the words "a perfect fertilizer."

"This one was about to come around here with a 12-gauge shotgun," Ruth said. "I persuaded him not to."

"Good idea," Rhodes said. He looked at his watch. "You're early."

Ruth smiled. "I've learned that it's not a bad idea to be a little early when it's you I'm backing up."

Rhodes looked at her prisoner. "You have a key to that storeroom?"

He stared back, saying nothing. His eyes looked as hard as marbles.

"If you don't let me in there, I'm going to get a warrant and come back with an axe," Rhodes said.

"I got a key," the man said. His voice was hoarse, and he sounded as if he might have a bad cold.

"Reach for it very carefully and toss it on the ground," Rhodes said.

He did what he was told. Rhodes picked up the key and opened the storeroom.

"I bet you one thing," Lawton said. "I bet those two ain't had a bath since the Carter administration."

Hack put down the hamburger he had brought in from the Bluebonnet. "I'd just as soon not talk about that right now," he said. "I'm tryin' to eat my lunch."

"How much dope you reckon they had in that storeroom?" Lawton asked Rhodes, who was also eating.

"Four or five pounds," Rhodes said. "Not cleaned or anything. That's counting seeds and stems."

"You can put in the papers that it has a street value of a million dollars," Hack said. "These days, if it don't have a

97

street value of a million dollars, it don't even rate the front page."

Actually, Rhodes had been disappointed with the find. It was certainly more than he had expected, in one way, but it was much less in another. There wasn't a trace of a refrigerator or a TV set, no old furniture, no tools, nothing that might have come from the burgled houses. The two men, brothers named Burl and Lonnie, swore they had no idea about any burglaries, no idea about the whereabouts of any green truck, and in fact no idea at all about how the dope could have gotten into their barn.

Rhodes figured they would change their minds about the dope, but he was pretty sure they were telling the truth about all the rest. When he brought up the dead woman, they had almost panicked. They knew that they were in trouble because of the marijuana, but murder was something even they didn't want to get mixed up in. Either they were excellent actors, or they were mostly innocent. Rhodes believed the latter.

He was curious about the marijuana, though. It wasn't often that much dope turned up in such a small, out-of-the-way county. He had encountered a large quantity of it only once before, and he wondered if these two had any connection with a man named Rapper, who had been behind the other deal. He hoped not. He didn't want to see Rapper back in Blacklin County anytime soon.

"We been goin' over that computer list of the people who bought the trucks," Hack said, folding up the paper that had held his burger and collecting the little cardboard containers from the French fries. "It came in with the mail. Not a single familiar name, and no address even close to here."

"Keep looking," Rhodes said. "You might find something."

"All right," Hack said. "We got something else for you, too. Calls came in from the Storm and the West families about those funeral registers."

"What about them?"

"They looked at 'em."

98

Rhodes got a grip on his patience. "That's all they did, just look?"

"Well," Hack said grudgingly, "they did say they noticed one thing."

Rhodes leaned forward in his chair. "What?"

"Wasn't much of anything," Hack said.

"Tell me anyway," Rhodes said.

"See, we don't think it amounts to anything," Lawton said. "We been talkin' it over, and we think—"

"Tell me anyway," Rhode said again, his voice hard.

"It's just that both of the families said there was names of people on there that they didn't know," Hack said. "I don't see how—"

"What were the names?"

"You don't have to get so snippy about it," Hack said. "I got 'em written down here somewhere." He began to ruffle through a stack of papers that he had jumbled in front of the radio. "Here they are. The Wests say they ain't ever heard of Mr. and Mrs. Jeffrey Sheldon or Sammie Faye Woods. And the Storms never heard of Sammie Faye or Mrs. and Mrs. Johnathan Spence."

Rhodes slammed his hand down on the desktop. "That's it!" he said. "Sammie Faye Woods!"

"Why is she it?" Hack said.

"The same person going to view both bodies, and the families never even heard of her. She must be the one who's doing the stealing," Rhodes said.

"See, that's what you can get by jumpin' to conclusions," Lawton said. "That's what Hack and I were sayin'. She didn't do anything."

"How do you know?" Rhodes said.

" 'Cause she's been around this county for eighty-five years," Hack said. "She goes to the funeral home just about ever' day to see who's there. She thinks it might be somebody she knows. You can ask Mr. Ballinger about her. He knows her. Ever'body knows about how she likes to go to funerals and see the bodies."

"I think I've heard about her," Rhodes admitted.

"Sure you have. Ever'body has," Lawton said.

"What about the other couples they never heard of?" Rhodes said. "There might be something in that."

"You can study on it if you want to," Hack said. "I don't see it myself."

Rhodes stared at the list. "I still think there's something to this. What else could there be?"

"You're the sheriff," Hack reminded him. "By the way, that Washburn fella's comin' in at four o'clock. Said it was the soonest he could make it. All Ruth told him was that it had something to do with the burglary of his property at the lake. You gonna talk to him?"

"Yes," Rhodes said. "I'll be here. It'll take me that long to go over that list of truck buyers."

"Won't help none to look at it," Hack said.

"Probably not," Rhodes said. "But we'll see."

Chapter 11

WASHBURN TURNED OUT to be a large man with a full black beard with hardly a touch of gray in it despite the fact that he was almost as old as Rhodes. He wore jeans and a white shirt. He told Rhodes that he was a teacher.

"At a community college in Houston," he said. "I teach American history and world history, not that anyone enrolls for world history anymore. They all think it's too tough for them, and it is. The only kind of serf they've ever heard of is spelled s-u-r-f, and they know they can find it at Galveston. Half the class drops out before the middle of the semester. Not that the students in American history are much better.

"But you didn't call me up here to listen to me talk about my job or my classes. The deputy said it was something about the burglary. I don't mind telling you that I hope you've recovered some of my things. I didn't have nearly enough insurance. I moved a lot of stuff in after my last renewal, and I never thought to notify anybody. Hell, my VCR alone was worth—"

"Excuse me, Mr. Washburn," Rhodes said, interrupting the flow of the man's talk. "You were called about the burglary, that's true, but it's something related to the burglary, not the burglary itself.''

"Related? You mean you called me all the way up here, a three-hour drive, just to talk about something *related*. This had better be good, Sheriff.''

"It's about a Mrs. Clayton," Rhodes said. "Sula Clayton.''

"Ah,'' Washburn said.

"You know her, I think," Rhodes said.

"I might.''

"Her husband seemed to think you knew her pretty well.''

"Ha. Her husband. A salesman. You know what e.e. cummings called a salesman, Sheriff Rhodes?''

Rhodes had to admit that he didn't know.

"He said, 'A salesman is an it that stinks.' ''

"He seemed all right to me," Rhodes said. "He didn't try to sell me anything.''

"You just weren't with him long enough. He'd have gotten around to it sooner or later.''

"He doesn't sell life insurance. And from what you were just telling me, you could have used a little better homeowner's policy.''

"Not from him I couldn't. What a twerp.''

It had been a long time since Rhodes had heard anyone called a twerp.

"What about his wife?" he said.

"His wife was different," Washburn said.

"Different in what way?''

"She was a sensitive, understanding woman. . . . Listen, Sheriff, I know Clayton must've told you about me and his wife. So what? Maybe we met here a time or two when he was off selling some kind of piddling group policy to a bunch of yuppies who make a living peddling General Motors stocks. I don't see what that has to do with the burglary of my lake house.''

"It doesn't have a thing to do with it," Rhodes said. "It might have something to do with Mrs. Clayton's murder, though.''

Washburn sucked in his breath, and Rhodes thought for a

102

minute he wasn't ever going to let it out again. When he finally did, it came out in brief puffs. Rhodes decided that if ever a man was surprised, Washburn was surprised.

When he could talk again, Washburn said, "Mrs. Clayton's been murdered?"

"Yes," Rhodes said. They still hadn't received the dental records, but Rhodes was certain he wasn't telling a lie.

"Who did it?" Washburn said. "Was it that son of a bitch Clayton? If it was him, I'll—"

"We don't know yet who did it," Rhodes said. "Clayton seemed to think it was you."

"That son of a bitch."

"His theory was that she drove down here to meet you but then came to her senses. And when she told you that she had to go back to her husband, you killed her."

"That son of a bitch."

Washburn was getting repetitive and not providing any useful information.

"When was the last time you saw her?" Rhodes asked.

"Right after Christmas. I had some time off from school and I came down for a weekend. She was able to get away for a day or two."

"Did her husband know about that?"

"He might have known. Sula thought he suspected."

Rhodes thought that the Christmas episode, assuming that it actually took place, might have been what Clayton and his wife had words about at the New Year's Eve party before she disappeared.

"You didn't start back to school until after New Year's, did you?" he said.

"No. We didn't register until a couple of weeks ago. But I had to do some things in the office, attend a workshop, stuff like that. I couldn't get back up here."

Rhodes could check on those things, or some of them. There would be a security office at the school. "You haven't heard from Mrs. Clayton since Christmas then?"

"That's right. I wondered if something had gone wrong at home. She usually would have given me a call by now. But I didn't think it would be anything like this."

103

"All right," Rhodes said. He didn't know what else to say. Washburn had been honest enough about his relationship with the dead woman, hadn't tried to hide anything. And his surprise on hearing about her death had not been faked. Rhodes was sure of that. "You think you could stay around a couple of days in case I have some more questions for you?"

"I have a class tomorrow at nine-thirty. I could call someone and ask him to take it. I don't know about Wednesday though."

"Maybe by then this will be settled," Rhodes said. He had already let Clayton go home, but he wasn't going to let Washburn off so easily. He wished he had Clayton back, too. At least he had Burl and Lonnie safely locked away. He would have to talk to them a bit more, too, but he'd give them a day or so in the cell to soften them up, assuming two such hardcases could ever be softened.

"I brought a folding cot," Washburn said. "I suppose I could sleep out at the lake tonight. I didn't want to drive back anyway."

"That sounds fine," Rhodes said. "I'll get in touch with you tomorrow."

Washburn shook hands and left.

"Well, how about that one?" Rhodes said.

Hack, who had as usual been bent over the radio pretending to be invisible, turned around. "Sounds all right to me. He was really surprised."

"Sounded that way, all right."

"What do you mean, *sounded*?"

"Remember what you said about being *too* surprised?"

"Yeah, but this wasn't the same kind of thing as being too surprised."

"How could you tell?"

"I could just tell," Hack said. "Trust me."

"The check is in the mail," Rhodes said.

"We're from the government. We're here to help you," Hack said.

"I am not a bimbo," Rhodes said.

"I never said you was," Hack told him. "That Miz Clayton, now . . ."

"Yes, she might be a different story," Rhodes said. "I think I'll talk to Mrs. McGee about her one more time."

"You think she knows any more than she's already told?"

"You never can tell. It won't hurt to pay her another little visit tomorrow."

"You find out anything from that list of folks who bought those trucks?"

Rhodes admitted that he hadn't. "Some were sold in Texas, some in California. Some were sold in lots, some were sold to individuals. It would take forever to trace them all down. But you were right about one thing. There's no one from around here on the list."

"Didn't think there would be. What about that other list? It was a whole lot shorter."

"I think there's something we can do about it, too. It may be nothing, or it may be just a coincidence, but it'll give us something to work on."

"Who's us?"

"Ivy and me."

"You gonna make her a deputy?"

"The deputies have plenty to do, and this should be an easy job. She's been a help to me before, and she might even enjoy it."

"But o' course it's a highly secret undercover job and you ain't about to tell us lower-level employees what it's all about."

"That's right," Rhodes said.

"Bull corn," Hack said, and turned back to face his radio.

"Do you think you can get the morning off tomorrow?" Rhodes asked Ivy that night. They were having supper at the Jolly Tamale, located just outside Clearview on the road to the lake. Having driven past it several times in the last few days, Rhodes had developed a craving for Mexican food.

"Why?" Ivy said. She was having the Number One, which consisted of a tamale, an enchilada, a taco, rice, and beans.

"To do a little secret undercover work," Rhodes said. He

was having the Number Two, which was just like the Number One, with the addition of guacamole salad. He liked guacamole, though he suspected that it was fattening.

"Sounds interesting," Ivy said, taking a bite from the enchilada. She chewed thoughtfully. "What kind of undercover work?"

Rhodes told her.

Ivy put down her fork and took a drink of the ice water the Jolly Tamale thoughtfully provided for all its customers. The hot sauce often required several refills of the water glass with each meal.

"Let me get this straight," Ivy said, putting down the water glass. "You want me to spend the morning lying in a coffin?"

"Well," Rhodes said. "Maybe not the entire morning."

"I'm not sure I want to spend even a few minutes doing it." She looked in Rhodes's eyes. "You're not much of a practical joker, I know that much."

"I'm not joking."

Ivy smiled. "I didn't think you were. Did you talk to Judge Parry today?"

Rhodes said that he had.

"And February twenty-seventh's all clear?"

Rhodes said that it was.

"You're not planning to bump me off in some bizarre premature burial plot, are you?"

Rhodes laughed. "It's nothing like that." He explained what he had in mind.

Ivy was dubious. "It's too late to get anything in the newspaper about it," she said.

"I called the radio station," Rhodes said. "Right after I cleared it with Clyde Ballinger."

"You called the radio station?"

Rhodes nodded.

"And you've already cleared it with Clyde Ballinger?"

Rhodes nodded again.

"Pretty sure of yourself, weren't you?"

"It's not that," Rhodes said. "It's just that I thought this was a good idea. Or at least *an* idea. I feel like I need to

106

solve one of these crimes, at least, and this is my best shot. If you don't want to do it, I can—"

"I didn't say I wouldn't do it. I'm just not too keen on the idea of lying in a coffin while I'm still alive. I'm not even sure I'm going to like it very much after I'm dead."

"I understand," Rhodes said. "I'll just ask Ruth Grady if she can do it. She might not like it any better than you do, but—"

"Hush," Ivy said. "I'll do it."

"I thought you would," Rhodes said.

She kicked his shin under the table. "Who do I get to be?"

"Miss Olivia Swain, one of Clearview's richest citizens," Rhodes told her. "A credit to her community."

"At least there's that," Ivy said.

Rhodes could hear the radio squawking while he paid the check. He asked Ivy to go out and respond to the call. She had learned to operate the radio the first time she rode in the patrol car, and Hack was used to hearing her answer calls.

"What's up?" Rhodes asked when he joined her a minute or two later.

"He wouldn't exactly say. He just told me to have you get out to the lake to Mrs. McGee's place as soon as you could. He said Ruth Grady was already on the way."

Rhodes climbed in the car, slammed the door, and put on his seat belt.

"Does this mean we get to use the siren?" Ivy said.

"I suppose it does," Rhodes said. He turned on the bubble lights and the siren.

"I think this must be the best part of your job," Ivy said. "Getting to turn on the siren and make everyone get out of the way."

"You'll notice that not everyone does," Rhodes said, swinging out to pass a slow-moving Chevrolet driven by a man who sat bolt upright with both hands holding the steering wheel in a death grip.

"He probably thought you were going to arrest him," Ivy said.

107

"I probably should," Rhodes said. "Someone's going to run right up his tailpipe some night. But I don't have time for him right now."

"What's the rush?"

"When Hack won't tell me what's going on over the radio, that means there's something happening that he doesn't think I'd want the whole county to know. He could use the code numbers, but everybody who owns a scanner has a code book."

"If he won't tell you what's happening, how can you know how to respond?"

"I always respond the same way. Very carefully. When you don't know exactly what's happening, you have a tendency to be extra careful."

"I hope you always are," Ivy said.

"Don't worry. I am." They turned off the main road and onto the winding way to Mrs. McGee's house. "We may beat Ruth there, since we were already so close. I want you to stay in the car. Don't even think about getting out."

"I won't."

"Unless I need you, of course. I'll let you know. Mrs. McGee could be hurt or something."

"I'll do whatever you say."

Rhodes hoped she was telling the truth. There was no need for her to get involved in whatever was coming up. He hadn't told her the complete truth about the radio call. About the only reason Hack would not have told him what was going on—knowing that Ivy was in the car—was that it was something quite serious, probably involving violence.

Rhodes turned off the siren and slowed to make the turn to Mrs. McGee's. The headlights illuminated the dark figure of a man standing in the middle of the road. Rhodes hadn't been going fast, and his sudden application of the break brought the car to an instant stop.

Rhodes cursed the seat-belt law under his breath. There were plenty of lawmen who simply ignored it, and he didn't blame them. Trying to stop a car, open the door, get out, and draw a weapon was hard enough. Add in the difficulty of getting out of the seat belt, and you had a real problem.

108

Somehow he managed it and came out of the car with a .38 in his hand.

"Don't shoot me, for God's sake," Washburn said. He was standing in front of the car with his hands raised. "I've already been shot at once."

Rhodes relaxed, but only a little. "Who shot at you?" he said. He kept the pistol pointed at Washburn.

"Somebody in that house there." Washburn pointed toward Mrs. McGee's house. "I was going to try to borrow a couple of blankets. I forgot to bring any for my cot, and it's pretty cold tonight."

Rhodes was still wearing his down jacket. He became suddenly conscious of the cold night air creeping in under it. The sky was absolutely clear, and the stars sparkled white high above them.

"Somebody shot at you because you tried to borrow some blankets?" Rhodes said.

"I didn't even get to ask. I just got about halfway across the yard when they opened up on me. Blam! Blam! Blam!"

"How'd you get in touch with my office?"

"Would you believe I brought a phone? Forgot the blankets and brought a phone. I was bringing in a few things to replace what was stolen, so I brought a phone and a few cooking pots. I thought . . . say, could I put my hands down now?"

Rhodes heard a siren in the distance. He knew that Ruth Grady was nearly there. "Sure," he said. He holstered his pistol. "Let's wait here for my deputy, and then we'll see what we can figure out."

Ruth stopped her car right behind the one Rhodes was driving. She had turned off her siren, but like Rhodes left the bubble lights on. They sent red and blue gleams bouncing off the black trunks of the bare trees. She got out of the car with her sidearm drawn, but Rhodes told her she wouldn't need it.

"There's been a little shooting," he said. "But it's all over, I think."

"What happened?" she said.

Rhodes told her.

109

"You think it was Mrs. McGee?"

"Maybe," Rhodes said. "We'll see."

He turned to Washburn. "You have a heater in your house?"

"Central heat. Those thieves didn't take the heating unit. I guess it was too big."

"Well, then, you better just turn it up high and sleep without the blankets tonight. My deputy will drive you over."

"My car's right over there," Washburn said. "I can get home all right." He shook his head. "I just stopped here because I saw the lights on. I didn't think there would be many people at home this time of year. Heck, I thought I was lucky to see a light."

Rhodes told Ruth to follow Washburn. "No sense in taking chances," he said.

Washburn saw the logic of it and went to get his car.

While Ruth was escorting Washburn home, Rhodes explained the situation to Ivy.

"Does this have anything to do with the murder out here?" she asked.

"That's what we'll try to find out," Rhodes said.

Chapter 12

THEY DROVE UP to Mrs. McGee's. There were still lights on in the house, and no sign of anyone prowling around the place. Rhodes had already decided to take Ivy in with them. She had proved to be an adept questioner, and she knew when to keep quiet. Besides, he certainly wasn't going to leave her out in the car. He and Ruth parked the county cars side by side and they all trooped up to the porch.

Rhodes knocked on the door.

"Who's there?" Mrs. McGee's voice asked.

"Sheriff Rhodes."

"I thought I saw those funny-colored lights. Just a minute."

The door opened. "Come on in. Quick, now. Heat's getting out."

The three of them crowded inside. Rhodes introduced Ivy.

"Pleased to meet you," Mrs. McGee said.

She was even more wrapped up than she had been the last time Rhodes saw her. She still wore the knit cap, but the afghan had been replaced by several sweaters and a heavy black coat that dragged the floor. Rhodes could see the sweaters because Mrs. McGee hadn't buttoned the coat in front. She looked like a stuffed doll with too much stuffing. The heat in the room was almost stifling. Rhodes had to resist the urge to take off his down jacket.

"I understand there was a little shooting out here," he said.

"Sit down, sit down," Mrs. McGee said.

Ruth and Ivy sat on a small couch. Rhodes and Mrs. McGee sat in the rockers, while Rhodes pulled his back from the fire.

"About that shooting, now," he said.

"Told you I could take care of myself," Mrs. McGee said. "Prowlers come snoopin' around here, they better watch out. I can take care of myself."

"I don't think it was a prowler, Mrs. McGee," Rhodes said.

She looked up at him from under the low rim of the knit cap. "Shows what you know about it. It was prowlers, all right."

She seemed very sure of herself. Rhodes asked her why.

"Came creepin' down the road in the dark, that's why. Who else would it be, anyhow?"

"The burglars had a van," Rhodes said. "You didn't see a van, did you?"

"It was dark. But I heard a car door slam, and when I looked out there was somebody slippin' up on the house. It was a prowler, all right."

Rhodes nodded. "I can see why you might think that, but you can't just open fire on everyone who comes toward your house after dark. This time you made a mistake. You almost killed one of your neighbors."

Mrs. McGee seemed to shrink inside her wrappings. "I thought it was a prowler," she said. "You aren't going to have to run me in, are you?"

"Not this time. But if you hear any more prowlers, try to make sure they really are prowlers. We don't need any more shootings out here than we have already."

"I didn't mean to hurt anybody."

"You didn't. This time. But next time might be different."

112

"It won't happen again," she said. "But it's not easy to tell who's creepin' up on you. If I hadn't seen those red and blue lights, I might've even shot at you."

"I'm glad you didn't," Rhodes said.

"I am, too, I'd hate to shoot the sheriff or his lady friend." She glanced at Ruth. "Or his deputy."

"You don't have more than one handgun lying around here, do you?" Rhodes asked.

"No," she said, too quickly. "Just the one."

"I'm not going to take your protection," Rhodes said.

Mrs. McGee didn't say anything.

"The man you almost shot was named Washburn," Ruth Grady said from her seat on the couch. "Do you know him?"

"Humph," Mrs. McGee said. The look on her face indicated that she was acquainted with the man but didn't consider him a friend.

"Has he been to your house before?" Rhodes asked.

"I wouldn't let him in if he came," Mrs. McGee said. "Just as well I took a shot at him, if it was him I shot at."

"Why?" Ruth said.

"Humph."

"You've seen him around the Clayton place, I bet," Rhodes said. "Is that right?"

Mrs. McGee looked at him shrewdly. "How do you figure?"

"It's no big secret that he and Mrs. Clayton . . . uh, liked each other," Rhodes said.

Ivy stifled a laugh. Rhodes looked at her sideways, but she had assumed a serious expression. Or maybe she hadn't almost laughed after all.

"I knew they did," Mrs. McGee said. "I told you I'd never seen those Claytons, but I guess I lied. I've seen her over there, and that Washburn sneakin' around like he hoped there wasn't nobody watchin' him. But there was, all right."

Rhodes was beginning to think that Mrs. McGee saw a lot more from her porch and her windows than she had let on at first. He wasn't surprised. Living all alone, away from the town, she might have become more interested in the comings and goings of her neighbors than in the daily soap operas on television.

"So you knew they were . . . ah, fooling around?"

Again the stifled laugh. Rhodes resolutely kept his eyes on Mrs. McGee.

"I knew, all right. It wasn't any of my business, but I knew. They had a fallin' out not so long ago, though."

"A falling out?"

"A fight. It was a loud one, too, or else I wouldn't've heard it all the way over here. What with the trees and all, you can hardly ever hear what's goin' on around you. But I heard this one."

"What was the trouble?" Rhodes asked. It was getting very, very hot in the room. He felt a rivulet of sweat trickle down from his hair to his cheek just in front of his right ear.

"I can't tell you that. They were loud, but all I could tell was that they were yellin'. Couldn't make out the words, but I could tell they were mad at each other."

"How about Mr. Clayton? You told me you never saw him either."

"Never did. Hardly ever saw her, for that matter, so I didn't lie too bad. Just once or twice, out in the yard. Never saw him though."

"You're sure."

"I'm sure."

"About this argument between Mrs. Clayton and Washburn. When was that?"

"I told you. Not so long ago."

"I meant, how long. A month? Two months?"

"It might've been around New Year's. I don't know for sure. I don't keep up much with the days anymore."

If she was even close, it meant that both Washburn and Clayton had argued with Mrs. Clayton around the same time, one of them in Dallas, and one of them here. And that shortly after the arguments, Mrs. Clayton had been killed and wrapped up in duct tape. Washburn was definitely taking on the aspect of a serious suspect in the case.

While Rhodes was thinking about that, Mrs. McGee

looked over at Ruth and Ivy. "I hope you two ladies are warm enough," she said.

"Oh yes," Ivy said. "We're fine."

"I have a throw in the other room," Mrs. McGee said. "You could wrap up in it if you wanted to."

"No, thank you," Ivy said. "I'm fine. Really."

"Don't see how you could be, in that skimpy little coat. This is the kind of weather that calls for something heavy."

"I guess I'm just warm-natured," Ivy said.

"I was, too, when I was younger," Mrs. McGee said.

Rhodes was not following the conversation. He was wondering about Mrs. Clayton and why she had been stripped after she was shot—or before she was shot—and about the duct tape. It didn't make any kind of sense.

"I guess that's all I need to ask you about tonight, Mrs. McGee," he said. "Just don't go shooting at anybody from now on. Give my office a call, and we'll get someone out here to deal with any prowlers you hear creeping up on you."

"You better get here plenty fast," she said.

"Don't worry. We will." Rhodes got up. Ivy and Ruth followed suit.

"I hope you all don't catch your deaths in those outfits," Mrs. McGee said. "You ought to wrap up better in this weather."

They thanked her for the advice as she ushered them quickly out the door and shut it firmly behind them. The outside air, after the time spent inside the nearly suffocating heat of the room, had a bracing effect, and they all inhaled deeply, pulling the cold into their lungs.

"Wow," Ruth said as they walked to the cars. "I thought I'd die in there. I'd hate to have to pay her gas bill."

"She told me that your blood thins out when you get old," Rhodes said. "Maybe she's right. Who knows?"

"Do you think it's safe to leave her there with a gun?" Ivy said.

"I hope so, but I never thought she'd actually shoot at anyone in the first place. Guess I was wrong."

"Don't you think it might be a good idea to take her gun,

then? And I think she has another one, or more than one."
Ivy sounded very concerned.

"I think you could be right about that," Rhodes said.
"But look at it this way. If I take her gun, what security does
she have? There have been a lot of burglaries in the neighborhood lately and one murder. She's an old woman living
alone, no one close by, no relatives anywhere around."

"There are lots of people in that situation," Ivy said.
"She's not unique, and I'll bet most of the others don't have
guns. Besides, you have patrols in the area, don't you?"

"That's not the point," Rhodes said. "She needs that gun
to think she's safe. It's like the security blanket that kid in
Peanuts carries. If we parked a car in front of her house, she
wouldn't feel as safe as she does with that gun."

"Nobody ever got shot with a security blanket," Ivy said.

Rhodes looked at Ruth, who gazed off at the waters of the
lake, which were reflecting the light of the stars.

"I'm getting cold," he said. "Let's go back to town."

They got in the cars and left.

"What's on TV tonight?" Ivy asked as they drove back
toward Clearview.

"The Black Swan," Rhodes said. "Tyrone Power at his
best."

"Does he play the swan?"

"He plays a pirate," Rhodes said.

"Is this one of those good pirate movies, like the ones we
used to see when we were kids? Swordfights, cannons, and
all that?"

"Exactly."

"Colorized?"

"No, thank goodness. This one was filmed in color to
begin with. You'll be able to tell the difference, I promise."

"Good." There was a long pause. "You know, you look
a little bit like Tyrone Power. Did I ever tell you that before?"

Rhodes laughed. *"Nobody* ever told me that before."

"Well, you do."

"Watch the movie, then tell me that again. Tyrone doesn't

have a single gray hair, and he doesn't need to watch his waistline. He even has a mustache.''

"Well, you look like Tyrone Power when he didn't have a mustache.''

"Keep it up,'' Rhodes said. "I might even start to believe it.''

"I'm sorry I said that about the security blanket,'' Ivy said. It sounded like a change of subject, but Rhodes knew that it wasn't. Not really.

"Don't be sorry. You had a valid point. I know I'm taking a risk. It's the same one I took the first time I saw Mrs. McGee with a pistol. Washburn almost got killed because I let her keep it then. I'm just hoping that she's learned a lesson.''

"The first time?''

"I knew she had that pistol earlier. Ruth and I saw it when I talked to her about the burglaries.''

"What if she'd killed someone with it?''

"I would have been guilty of really bad judgment. But I'd do the same again. In fact, I just did. I don't see her as the kind of person who'd kill someone.''

"Unless it was an accident.''

"That's right, unless it was an accident.''

"Well, you're the one who has to live with his judgments.''

Rhodes let it go at that. It had been a long day.

Ruth would have let Hack know the outcome of their trip to the lake, but during a commercial break in the movie, Rhodes called the jail. There was always the chance that Burl and Lonnie had confessed or that there was some other minor matter that might need his attention. Hack didn't like to bother him if it wasn't absolutely necessary.

Ivy was in the kitchen making popcorn. Rhodes had bought a dry popper, one that required no oil and no butter. The popcorn didn't taste like much, but at least he knew he wasn't getting any calories or cholesterol.

No one had confessed, however, and there wasn't much going on.

"We did get a call from one of the honky-tonks," Hack said.

Rhodes had explained to Hack more than once that there was no such thing as a honky-tonk anymore. There were clubs—like there were no trash collectors anymore, just sanitary engineers. Hack paid him no attention.

"What was the trouble?" Rhodes said. On the telephone, Hack was usually more forthcoming about matters than he was in person.

"Twila Faye Eckert called in about a man rumagin' around in her purse. Said she caught him red-handed." Twila Faye was a well-known local character, one who spent more time on the inside of the various "clubs" in Blacklin County than she did on the outside of them. In one way or another, her name figured in several complaints over the years.

"Who took care of it?" Rhodes asked.

"Buddy went out. He's dealt with Twila Faye before."

Buddy was a solid deputy, and Rhodes was confident he had handled things well. "Any arrests?"

"Nope."

"Any trouble?"

"Nope. Turned out that Twila Faye had cold-cocked the guy already. He was laid out on the floor when Buddy got there. She hit him with a bottle of Coors Lite, right behind the ear."

"How badly was he hurt?"

"He was okay. He came to while Buddy was there. Turned out he had good reason for goin' through Twila Faye's purse."

"Well?"

"They been livin' together for five months in her house. He wasn't feelin' too well and wanted to go home, so he started lookin' through her purse for the house key. She wanted to stay and have a good time. Said all he cared about was watchin' TV, and she wanted to have a little fun while she was still young."

Rhodes knew that Twila Faye was forty-five if she was a day. "Did anybody want to file on anybody else?"

"Nope. The old boy said he'd stay and have another beer

118

if Twila Faye'd go home after that. She said she would, so they were all friends again when Buddy left.''

''And that's it for the night?''

''It's Monday,'' Hack said.

''I'm going to be busy for a while in the morning, but I'll see you before noon,'' Rhodes told him. ''You can reach me at Ballinger's if there's trouble.''

''All right,'' Hack said. ''See you then.''

Rhodes hung up and went to eat dry popcorn and watch Tyrone Power win the love of Maureen O'Hara. He caught a glimpse of his reflection in the glass of a door as he passed.

Maybe there is a vague resemblance, he thought. Then he shook his head. No way.

Chapter 13

"SHE REALLY MAKES a nice corpse," Clyde Ballinger said as he and Rhodes stood looking at Ivy. "You'll notice I didn't skimp on the casket, either. This is one of our best. The finest steel." He knocked against it with his fist. "And that's real silk she's lying on. Not any of that polyester stuff that you get in the cheaper boxes."

"We don't want the sales pitch," Ivy said. She still had her eyes closed, but the fact that she had spoken spoiled the illusion she had created after Rhodes had helped her climb into the coffin. She had looked quite dead. With just the right amount of makeup—too much—and the appropriate pose, her hands crossed on her breast.

Rhodes took the folding chair that Ivy had climbed on and put it back with the others. "How long can you hold your breath?" he said.

"You should have asked me that sooner," Ivy said. "But I can probably do it long enough."

"Remember that no one's going to try to hurt you," Rhodes said. "They think you're dead already. And Clyde and I will be right here."

"I just want you to know that I like this even less than I thought I would," Ivy said.

"I really appreciate your doing it," Rhodes said.

"Probably not enough," she said. "You owe me one."

"Who's keeping score?"

"I am."

"You remember what to do?"

"I remember."

"It's nearly eight o'clock," Ballinger said. "Tom'll be opening the door soon."

"Let's go," Rhodes said. "We'll be watching," he called to Ivy.

There was no answer from the coffin.

Rhodes and Ballinger moved to the right side of the room, which was not a wall but a folding soundproof curtain. It could be folded back for really big crowds, but more often it was used as a wall between two smaller rooms.

Ballinger pushed the curtain a foot or so and they squeezed by. Then he pushed it up to the catch, but did not complete the connection.

"Let me stand there so I can see," Rhodes said.

Ballinger moved aside, and Rhodes pressed his face to the small crack. He had a good view of the dais and the coffin. As he watched, the recorded music came on. The song was "How Great Thou Art."

"When did you start that stuff?" Rhodes asked.

"It's very soothing," Ballinger said. "Besides, it saves money if the family doesn't want to hire an organist or singer."

"I'll tell you what," Rhodes said. "When my time comes, I want a piano player. I don't even want this stuff turned on."

"I guess that can be arranged," Ballinger said. His tone showed that his feelings were slightly injured.

"I want all fast music," Rhodes said. "Things like 'I'll Fly Away,' 'Beulah Land,' 'The Rock That Is Higher Than I,' 'When They Ring Those Golden Bells for You and Me.' And make sure the piano player gets them up to speed. None of that dragging like some of them do at funerals."

"I'll try to remember," Ballinger said. "It might be a while before you get here."

"I hope so. Maybe I better write it down."

"Somebody's coming in," Ballinger said. He pressed up next to Rhodes so that he could see through the crack.

An old woman entered the room. It was hard to say how tall she might have once been because her back was bent and she walked as if she were leaning over to look for something on the floor. She had on a black dress that reached low enough to cover the tops of her shoes and a crocheted black shawl. Her hair was white and thin, and she wore it combed close to the top of her head and caught in a knot at the back.

"Sammie Woods," Ballinger whispered. "She hasn't missed looking at a body in the last twenty years."

The old woman made her way carefully down to the dais and stood quietly, looking at Ivy. Then she looked around the room for the other mourners, as if she wondered where they all were. She moved as close to the coffin as she could, but she made no attempt to touch Ivy or to step up on the dais.

She stayed for around fifteen minutes, and after a while Rhodes noticed that she was swaying slightly in time to the music, which at that moment was "Rock of Ages."

Ballinger nudged Rhodes in the ribs. "See," he said. "Some people like it."

Rhodes didn't say anything because he thought he could hear someone else coming in. Sure enough, a man and a woman entered the room. The man was tall and distinguished-looking, sort of like George Sanders when he played The Saint, though not as he had looked in *The Black Swan*. The woman was short and dumpy, wearing a cheap black dress and crying into a handkerchief. The man was holding her arm and bending to whisper in her ear, but whatever he said only made her cry harder. Sammie Woods moved respectfully aside as they approached. She could tell real grief when she saw it.

The man and woman stood in front of the coffin, and the man moved his hand from the woman's arm to her shoulders, which were shaking from her crying. In an excess of grief, the woman pulled away from him and stepped up on the dais, bending over Ivy. It seemed to Rhodes, from where he was watching, that she was caressing Ivy's cheeks.

From here on, the plan was simple. If this couple was the same one who had come to view other bodies and used names with the initials "J.S." to sign the register, Rhodes believed that they would in some way remove the jewelry from the body, or in this case from Ivy. When they started to leave, Ivy would signal, and Rhodes would meet them in the hall.

Things did not go exactly according to plan, however. After about five minutes of nonstop mourning over the coffin, with Rhodes wondering how on earth Ivy was holding her breath that long, the woman stepped back. As the man put his arm around her again, there was a low moan from the coffin.

Three heads jerked up as if the bodies attached to them had been jabbed with cattle prods.

As the moaning continued, Ivy began to rise up stiffly from the coffin, her arms stretched straight in front of her.

Sammie Woods began backing up, knocking over three of the folding chairs before finally sitting down in one. She was moaning too by this time.

The man and the woman stood as if rooted in place for several seconds, then turned and started for the door.

Rhodes slapped the folding curtain about three feet and hurtled into the room. "Hold it!" he yelled.

The man looked back over his shoulder, saw Rhodes in pursuit, and shoved the woman aside. She tried to tackle Rhodes as he passed, but he eluded her groping arms and kept after the man.

By now Ivy was climbing out of the coffin. Sammie Woods was still moaning, but the moans were threatening to turn into screams. Ballinger ran into the room and began tussling with the woman on the floor.

When Rhodes got to the door, the man was retreating back into the room. Tom Skelly was in front of him, his hands up like a boxer's.

"Come on," Skelly said. "Just come right ahead. I'm ready for you. Come on."

123

Rhodes clapped the man on the shoulder. "I've got him now, Tom," he said. "You take care of Miss Woods."

The man made no attempt to resist. His shoulder felt almost boneless under Rhodes's hand. Ballinger had subdued the woman and seated her in a chair.

Ivy was standing by Sammie Woods, trying to explain what had been happening, but the old woman wasn't hearing her. Skelly finally took her by the arm and led her from the room.

Rhodes looked at Ivy.

She smiled. "I couldn't resist," she said.

The man and woman, a husband and wife named Melvin and Deanie Holcomb, were booked and jailed. Ruth Grady searched the woman and found the earrings that Ivy had been wearing, as well as the necklace, but the two would admit nothing else. They refused to say that they had taken anything from bodies in the past, though Rhodes was certain they had. They had signed the register this time as Mr. And Mrs. Johnny Simmons, and Rhodes was sure that an analysis of the handwriting would prove that they had signed the registers previously. Why they had such a fondness for the J.S. Combination, he didn't know. Maybe it reminded them of John Smith.

They also refused to give any address or place of residence, which bothered Rhodes some. What bothered him even more—or at least gave him cause to wonder—was the look on Burl and Lonnie's faces when Melvin was put into a cell. The look had not lasted long, and Rhodes might have doubted he saw it had he not been so certain he had. The look said as plain as words that Burl and Lonnie knew Melvin and wondered just what he was doing in jail.

When questioned later, everyone denied knowing everyone else, or even having seen each other before. Burl and Lonnie would also have denied knowing one another if it had been feasible.

"Jail's gettin' too full," Lawton said.

"Not full enough," Rhodes said. "We still don't have the burglars or the killer."

124

"We got the ones that Clyde was so worried about," Hack said. "Maybe now things will settle down for him."

"Not until we get the jewelry back," Rhodes said. "Those two don't seem inclined to tell where it is."

"They'll come around sooner or later," Lawton said. "This ain't exactly the Embassy Suites." As far as Rhodes knew, Lawton had never stayed in a motel or hotel. He had probably seen an advertisement on TV.

Rhodes wasn't so sure anyone would come around. As far as they had been able to discover, Burl and Lonnie had no previous records, not even for something like simple assault. The main thing they were concerned about was their dog, which Rhodes had assured them was being cared for. It had been taken to the county animal shelter, and they could have it when they got out.

Melvin and Deanie didn't have records, either, at least not in Blacklin County. Rhodes figured that when he checked they'd be clean elsewhere. If they were, it was going to be hard to get anything more than a probated sentence for either of them, even though robbing a corpse was a pretty disgusting crime. Somehow, though, they were tied in with Burl and Lonnie, which was interesting and probably meaningful. Now if only Rhodes could figure out what it meant.

"You gonna hire Ivy on as a deputy?" Hack asked.

"I don't think so," Rhodes said. "She doesn't follow orders too well."

"I sure wish I coulda seen that," Hack said. "It musta been quite a sight, her risin' up out of the casket box like that, moanin' and takin' on like a ghost."

"Yeah," Lawton said. "And I expect Sammie Woods won't ever go to look at another body as long as she lives. Did they ever get her calmed down?"

"Pretty well," Rhodes said. "Tom Skelly's good at things like that. But I'll say one thing. I think she was paler than Ivy when the whole thing was over. She's still not sure whether Ivy was part of a plan or just a body that the doctor made a mistake about."

"Tell her about embalmin'," Hack said. "After you embalm somebody, they won't be doin' any risin' up."

"Right now I need to rise up and go have a talk with Washburn," Rhodes said, getting out of his chair. "He said he had a phone out there, so give me a call if anything comes up."

"Yeah," Lawton said. "Like a jail break, with all these prisoners we got in here."

"If that happens," Rhodes said, "I don't even want to know about it."

It was still cold, but the temperature was moderating. The sunshine helped a lot. Still, it wasn't warm enough for sitting outside, and Rhodes didn't see Mrs. McGee on her porch. He drove by her house slowly, but caught no sight of her.

Washburn's house was a simple white frame, recently painted. Rhodes knocked on the door, and Washburn invited him in.

"I haven't had anything to eat," Washburn said. "No stove to cook on, no refrigerator to keep things in. It's a wonder they didn't take the plumbing fixtures, too. I hope you're going to let me leave here today. Besides, I need to teach those classes tomorrow. I am going to get to leave, right?"

"That all depends," Rhodes said.

Because of the beard it was hard to read Washburn's expression, but he looked a little odd to Rhodes. "Depends on what?" he said.

"On our getting a few things straight. First of all, let me ask you something I should have asked before. Is there a Mrs. Washburn?"

"No," Washburn said. "Why?"

"The mailbox," Rhodes said.

"Oh. Well, there was a Mrs. Washburn a few years ago, but that's all in the past. I didn't paint that on the mailbox, by the way. Some guys came through here doing it. Charged five dollars a box."

"So there wasn't any real reason for you not to see Mrs. Clayton—that is, no real reason if she hadn't been married."

"No. And since she and her husband were having trouble, I didn't see anything wrong with what we did."

126

"I understand that you and she had a big argument not so long ago."

"Who told you that?"

"I can't say. It's confidential."

"That meddling old McGee bat, I'll bet."

"Meddling?"

"What else could you call it? She's always slipping around, watching people, snooping through their yards. If that's not meddling, I don't know what is."

"I got the impression that she never even left her house," Rhodes said.

Washburn laughed. "That's the impression she wants you to get. She wants everyone to think she's a harmless little old lady, always sitting on her porch. It's just not true. Sula had me chase her out of the yard one time. I think she was trying to get a look in through the window to see what we were doing."

Rhodes sighed. He was used to being lied to, but he had really thought Mrs. McGee was telling him the truth. He was going to have to rethink his whole attitude toward her.

"We'll worry about her later," he said. "Just tell me what the argument was about."

"Look," Washburn said. "I argued with her about her husband. I thought she should get a divorce from him and live in Houston with me. It was obvious that they were never going to get along."

"When was this argument?"

Washburn slumped a bit. "All right. I was here after New Year's. That's when we had the argument. It must've been right before she got killed. But I didn't do it. Look, I don't need this. There aren't too many things that can get a teacher fired, but being involved in a murder might be one of them."

"Your job isn't one of the things that bothers me," Rhodes said. "Murder is."

"But I told you I didn't do it. Sure, I was here around that time, but I didn't do anything. We had an argument, I left. She said she was going to try to patch things up with her husband, and I told her it was a big mistake. We got a little

127

excited and maybe there was a little yelling. But that's all there was."

"Can you prove it?"

"I don't have to. I know that much about the law. After the argument, I went back to Houston. I can prove that."

Rhodes asked him about Burl and Lonnie and the Holcombs.

"Never heard of them," Washburn said.

Rhodes hadn't really thought he would have. "I'll probably need to talk to you again," he said. "You'd better call and see if you can get someone else to sit in on those classes for you tomorrow."

Washburn wasn't happy, but he said he'd try.

Chapter 14

RHODES WENT HOME after the interview with Washburn. He wanted to spend some time thinking about what he knew and what he didn't know as far as the murder and the burglaries were concerned.

He played in the yard with Speedo for a minute, then went inside to watch the Million Dollar Movie. Watching movies helped him think, and it didn't matter whether the movies were any good or not. In fact, it was usually better if they weren't any good. That way he didn't really try to follow them.

He had stopped on the way in and picked up a Number Two To Go at the Jolly Tamale. He heated it up and located a Dr Pepper. By then, the movie had already started, but that didn't really matter. It was *Man's Favorite Sport?*, which he had already seen numerous times before. He had long since decided that its principal virtue was Paula Prentiss, though even she wasn't up to the high standard she had set in *Where the Boys Are*. And she was wasting her time on Rock Hudson, through Rhodes had to admit he hadn't known that the first few times he'd seen the movie.

129

So while the man who knew everything about fishing but had never fished tried to work out his problems, Rhodes thought about his own difficulties. There was the dead woman, first of all. Wrapped in duct tape. Found in a house that had been burgled, like all the unoccupied houses in the neighborhood, by very neat burglars who apparently owned a U-Truck-'Em van, or at least had access to one.

Rhodes had seen the van, all right, up close and personal, but he hadn't seen the driver or the passenger. He knew more or less the direction the van had been headed in, but he hadn't been able to locate it. Instead, he'd located a marijuana stash. That didn't mean the van wasn't still in the same general area. There were plenty of places it could be hidden back in those boondocks. But all he'd come up with was Burl, Lonnie, and their stash.

Rhodes also had Melvin and Deanie—the people who were robbing the corpses—and was convinced that there was a connection between them and Burl and Lonnie. Rhodes just didn't know what the connection was, or whether it was meaningful.

There still might be something to tie Burl and Lonnie to the burglaries, if he could only figure out what it was. But could he tie them to the murder? He still didn't know if the murder had been done by the burglars or by someone else. If someone else, who was that? Both Washburn and Clayton were convincing in their protestations of innocence, but Washburn had already lied more than once about where he'd been and what he'd done.

Unfortunately, so had Mrs. McGee, a seemingly harmless little old lady who sat on her porch with a .357, had taken a shot at Washburn, and probably had a least one other gun in the house. She had made Rhodes believe that she never left her own front yard, but Washburn, who might or might not be lying, said that she was a snoop who even tried to peek in her neighbors' windows.

What if her other gun was a .38?

Rhodes took his paper plate into the kitchen, where he dumped it into the trash. He went back to the living room and stared at the ending of the movie without really seeing it. He was sure that he had all the pieces—or most of them, but he could see no way to put them together that made any sense.

It was time to go back to the jail.

Nothing had changed. Melvin and Deanie still maintained their silence, and Burl and Lonnie still wanted to see their dog.

"Anything new come up?" Rhodes asked.

"Nothin' much. Got a call from a lady over in the north part of town, said there was some boys shootin' birds out of all the trees in the neighborhood," Hack said. "Ruth went over to take care of it."

"What were they shooting with?"

"Just BB guns," Hack said. "Happens sooner or later after ever' Christmas. Their mamas and daddys tell those boys not to go shootin' the birds with their new guns, but they finally forget, or they just can't resist tryin' those guns out on somethin' besides a target."

"You're sure that's all there is to it?" Rhodes asked. Sometimes boys got .22s for Christmas, and the problems were multiplied. There had been no cases in Blacklin County of children killing their friends yet, despite a number of reports from around Houston, and Rhodes hoped the record would remain clean. When there were guns around the house, however, anything could happen.

"That's all there was," Hack said. "She didn't hear any loud shots or anything like that. Just saw the boys shootin' up in the trees with their BB rifles."

The trouble was, Rhodes thought, anyone could pick up a gun with ease, at a flea market or nearly anywhere else, these days. It was a thought that had occurred to him before and had given him an idea that he should follow up on.

"They still have that big flea market up around Dallas somewhere?" he asked Hack.

"I don't keep up with that stuff. I got all the junk I need already. You ought to ask Clyde Ballinger a question like that. Why? You thinkin' about gettin' rid of some of your stuff?"

"It might not be a bad idea," Rhodes said, thinking about Ivy's question to him about whether they would live in his house or hers. Either move would no doubt involve getting rid of a number of possessions. "I'm going over to the funeral home."

Ballinger was happy to tell Rhodes about the flea market. "I haven't been in a long time, though," he said. "When I first started going, I could find all kinds of good books there, but lately there hasn't been a thing worth buying. Seems like everybody's got these big thick books by Irving Wallace and Sidney Sheldon. Nobody even wants to sell you anything that doesn't have a cover price of four-fifty. All the good paperbacks, the ones that sold for twenty-five or thirty-five cents, you can hardly find those now'days unless you get lucky at a garage sale. Or maybe from some dealer that wants ten dollars for one of them."

Rhodes hadn't meant to get Ballinger started on his favorite topic. "I wasn't looking for books," he said.

"Well, if you do see any like these"—Ballinger waved a hand to indicate the books lining his shelves—"be sure to pick them up for me. Guys like Harry Wittington and Jim Thompson could tell a story in less than two hundred pages. They didn't need six hundred like everybody seems to now. And they were good stories, let me tell you. Not like most of this bloated stuff you read now."

"You say they get started on Thursday?" Rhodes said. He hated to interrupt, but it looked as if Ballinger was good for another three hours.

"Thursday afternoon. Used to, they didn't start selling until after noon on Sunday, but things got so big they had to start earlier and earlier. I doubt you'll be able to cover the ground in just an afternoon. What're you looking for, anyway?"

"I'm not exactly sure," Rhodes said.

"The Storms were by here today," Ballinger said. "They still aren't happy about Miss Storm's being buried without that jewelry. Have those Holcombs confessed yet?"

"Not yet," Rhodes said. "They haven't said anything at

all, aside from their names, and I'm not sure they're telling the truth about that."

It's too bad we can't go back to the old days," Ballinger said. "Not that the boys in the Eighty-seventh ever did anything vicious even in the old days. You know that series has been going on for over thirty years now? Anyway, Carella would never do anything to beat a confession out of anyone, but Hawes, maybe he would have. Back in the old days, I mean. Not now. But you take Lou Ford—he's the deputy in *The Killer Inside Me*—he'd do anything and just about did."

Ballinger had discussed his favorite book with Rhodes before. "I think sometimes the writers exaggerate the old days," Rhodes said, though he had heard stories about past sheriffs in Blacklin County who hadn't been averse to administering a few judicious blows with the rubber truncheon from time to time.

"Maybe they do exaggerate," Ballinger said, "but it makes a pretty good story when they do."

"Well, I'm not going to break out the battery cables and start in beating on people," Rhodes said. "We'll put the formal charges on the Holcombs and then get them a lawyer if they don't already have one. Maybe they'll talk to him. I can't even find out where they live."

"Aren't they on the tax rolls?"

"No, and they aren't in the phone book, either. But we'll find out where they come from sooner or later. I imagine that the rest of the loot will be right in the house."

"I wish you'd find it sooner," Ballinger said. "It'd do me a world of good with the Storms."

"When they come in again, tell them it's just a matter of time," Rhodes said.

"I'll do better than that," Ballinger told him. "I'll just send them right on to you and let you tell them."

"Thanks," Rhodes said.

That night he was fixing supper for himself and Ivy again. He had decided to keep it simple this time and make his specialty, which was what his daughter called beanie-weenie. She had also told him that it was only one step above bologna

133

as a gourmet dish, but at least it was something he could do without too much trouble.

He drained off the liquid from a can of pork-and-beans and dumped the beans in a cooking pot. Then he added ketchup, vinegar, Worchestershire sauce, butter, and dried onion flakes. He didn't measure any of the ingredients, going mostly by the way the mixture looked. When it got to be just about the right color, he cut up the wieners and dumped them in the pot as well. The secret, as he had told his daughter, was to use only Oscar Mayer wieners. They had just the right flavor to blend in with the other ingredients.

He turned on the fire under what he preferred to call barbecued franks and beans and stirred the mixture a few times. It looked fine to him. Add some corn bread and Dr Pepper, and you had a meal fit for a king. He hoped he had some corn bread mix in the house, he wasn't very good at making it from scratch. It fact, he wasn't very good at making it from a mix, either, but it usually turned out to be edible.

Ivy arrived just in time to save the corn bread from incineration and to stir the beans and franks one last time. Rhodes dipped his wooden spoon in for a taste and pronounced it ready.

"Well?" Rhodes asked after they had gotten seated and begun to eat.

"I have to admit that these are the best barbecued beans and franks I've ever tasted," Ivy said.

Rhodes assumed that she meant it as a compliment.

After they did the dishes, they discussed their marriage plans. Rhodes wanted to keep things simple.

"We'll just get ready and go to the judge and get married," he said. "I don't think we need to make any real plans."

"What about a honeymoon?" Ivy asked.

Rhodes admitted he hadn't thought about that.

"You should be able to get a few days off," she said. "When was the last time you took a vacation?"

He couldn't remember.

"I thought so. We could go somewhere like San Antonio

134

and spend a few days. There are a lot of things to do in a city like that, even in the winter.''

Rhodes was not overly fond of cities, winter or summer. "Well, maybe," he said. He didn't sound extremely enthusiastic, even to himself.

"Whatever happened to those people from this morning?" Ivy said, changing the subject, for which Rhodes was grateful.

"They still haven't admitted anything. I'm not sure we'll ever get them to talk," Rhodes said. Then he told her of his suspicion that the Holcombs might be connected in some way with Burl and Lonnie.

"Do you think they're related or just acquainted?"

Rhodes said that he didn't know. "I might be reading too much into just a look, but I think there's something to it."

"And you've never found that truck?"

"Not yet. We're still looking."

"What if the Holcombs owned the truck?"

Rhodes hadn't thought about that, but he was pretty sure there were no Holcombs on the list of buyers. It was something he could check, however. There had to be some good reason why they were keeping their address a secret. They didn't dress or act like they lived back in the boonies near Burl and Lonnie, but you could never tell. Maybe they did.

There was no movie on that Rhodes wanted to watch, and he didn't have anything on tape, so he decided to play a few of his old records. He and Ivy could sit around and talk some more, and maybe she would come up with some more ideas that would be useful to him. He located a copy of *Roy Orbison's Greatest Hits* and put it on the turntable. Rhodes didn't own up-to-date stereo equipment. In fact, his stereo was about as old as the record album. That was fine with Rhodes, who had a theory that old music from the fifties and early sixties sounded best on the small, tinny speakers used in automobiles of the day. Roy Orbison was probably an exception. Turned up to full volume, his voice could blast the speakers out of nearly anything. As Roy launched into a scratchy version of "Only the Lonely," Ivy apologized for getting carried away at the funeral home that morning.

135

"I just couldn't help myself," she said. "It was really spooky, lying there and pretending to be dead. I kept thinking of what it would feel like if the coffin lid were to be closed on me."

"I told you not to worry about that," Rhodes said.

"I think I read too much Edgar Allen Poe when I was a teenager," Ivy said. "And then that woman came in, crying and running her hands over me. That was the really strange part. I almost believed she was really grieving. And you couldn't believe the touch she had. I didn't even realize the first earring was gone until she started on the second one, and she might have gotten that one off without my knowing if she hadn't dropped part of it. She had to reach down for it and she jostled me."

"What I was wondering was how you could hold your breath so long," Rhodes said.

"I just had to take very shallow breaths when she'd go into a crying spell," Ivy said. "I was afraid she'd catch me."

"But you caught her instead. Clyde's pretty happy you did." Rhodes paused. "Of course, I'm afraid you set Miss Woods back a bit."

"I'm sorry about that. It was just so much like one of those old scary movies I couldn't resist, and it seemed like as good a signal as any. I hope she wasn't too scared."

"Clyde says she'll be all right. Maybe she can find some other way to spend her time now. I don't think she'll ever feel the same about funeral homes again."

Ivy laughed. "Me either."

Chapter 15

THEY GOT TO listen to most of the Orbison album before Hack called. "Sorry if I interrupted anything," Hack said, though his tone indicated that he wasn't sorry at all. "You better get out to the lake. There's some shootin' goin' on out there again around Miz McGee's."

"Who called?" Rhodes asked.

"Didn't say. Just said it sounded like a war had broke out."

"I'm on the way."

Ivy insisted on going, and Rhodes, against his better judgment, said that she could, even though the lake area was getting to be more and more like a firing range and you could never tell who might step in front of a bullet.

"You'll have to stay in the car," Rhodes told her, though he wasn't sure how much protection the car would provide.

"Siren again?" Ivy asked.

"Siren again," Rhodes said.

When they got to the lake, Mrs. McGee's house was ablaze with lights, though the houses all around were dark. Rhodes stopped the car, got out, and ran to Mrs. McGee's door. Ivy was right behind him, despite what he had told her.

Mrs. McGee met them at the door. "Come on in," she said. She still had on her cold-weather gear. Rhodes wondered if she slept in it.

"What's going on, Mrs. McGee?" Rhodes said as soon as they were inside.

"I don't know, Sheriff," she said. Her face looked haggard beneath the knit cap.

"Has there been more shooting?"

"I'm afraid there has," she said. She walked over to her rocker by the fire and sat down. She didn't invite Rhodes or Ivy to sit. She simply folded her hands in her lap and began rocking slowly back and forth.

Rhodes walked over to stand beside her. "Did you shoot anyone?" he asked.

Mrs. McGee shook her head. "Don't think so," she said.

"Did you shoot *at* anyone?"

Mrs. McGee continued to rock. "Maybe," she said.

Rhodes was beginning to get frustrated. "Maybe? How can you *maybe* shoot at someone?"

Ivy said, "Do you have any tea, Mrs. McGee? I'd surely like a cup of hot tea."

The old woman got up. "I'll fix you some," she said.

Rhodes watched her walk slowly to the kitchen. "All right," he said to Ivy. "I was starting to lean on her a little. It wasn't a good idea."

"No, it wasn't," Ivy said. "She's old, and she's a little confused. Give her time to think things over."

"I'm afraid if I give her too much time, she'll come up with a twisted version of the story," Rhodes said. In low tones he told Ivy of Washburn's comments on Mrs. McGee's behavior.

"You believe him?"

"I'm not sure who to believe anymore," Rhodes said. "All I know is that something funny's going on, but I'm not sure what it is."

They waited for Mrs. McGee while the incredible heat of the room began to make itself felt. Rhodes, who had noticed

138

a slight draft the first time he visited, now noticed one even more extreme. And there was hardly any wind.

He began to look around the room. Directly across from him was a shattered windowpane. The window was divided into four sections, and the glass in one section was almost completely missing. He turned and looked at the wall. There was what looked like a bullet hole there. To get to the bullet, he would have to remove that section of the wall. He didn't want to damage the bullet by digging for it like they did on television.

The bullet was concrete evidence of gunfire, even if Mrs. McGee had fired it herself, which didn't seem likely, given her preference for warmth and the fireside. Rhodes didn't think she would have gone outside to shoot back into the house, so someone must have been shooting at her.

Unless she was more clever than he thought, in which case she might have fired the bullet in order to make him think someone was trying to kill her. He didn't know why she might want to do that, but then he didn't know why anyone would want to kill her either.

He heard a kettle whistle in the kitchen, and Ivy went to help Mrs. McGee with the tea. Rhodes continued to study the room, but there didn't seem to be any other signs of a gun battle. He sat down in the rocker and waited for the tea. He hated tea.

When the two women returned, they were talking softly. Ivy was telling Mrs. McGee that tea was a wonderful drink for settling the nerves. They set the cups and teakettle down on an end table by the couch and poured three cups. Rhodes had been hoping they might forget him, but they hadn't. He would pretend to sip it without really drinking any. Ivy handed him his cup. It was thin china with painted roses.

"Mrs. McGee was just telling me what happened," Ivy said. "It's been a very unsettling experience for her."

"I'm sure it has," Rhodes said, pretending to sip the tea, which was much too hot. He wished he had a Dr Pepper.

They all sat down, Rhodes and Mrs. McGee in the rockers, Ivy on the couch. Rhodes had trouble balancing the cup and saucer, so he finally reach over and set it on top of the

Dearborn heater. The top of the stove was heavily insulated and remained cool, no matter how hot the fire might be.

"Maybe you'd like to tell me what happened now, Mrs. McGee," he said.

Her hands began to shake and the cup clattered against the saucer. "I was sitting right here," she said. "Right here in this chair. I was feeling a little cold, so I bent over to get closer to the fire."

Rhodes found it hard to imagine that anyone would want to get any closer to the fire. He could feel it right through his pants legs.

"That was when it happened," Mrs. McGee said.

"What happened?" Rhodes said.

"Someone shot at me!" Mrs. McGee's voice rose sharply on the second word. "I didn't really hear the shot, but I heard the window smash, and something hit the wall over there."

They both turned to look at the wall where Rhodes had spotted the bullet hole.

"What did you do then?" Rhodes said.

She looked at him accusingly. "Well, you'd got me so scared about hurting someone that I didn't have my pistol with me. It was in the bedroom. I went in there to get it."

"There was no more shooting?"

"Not right then."

"When, then?"

"When I went outside."

Rhodes could imagine what a target she must have made, silhouetted in the doorway. "You shot back?"

"I surely did. And got shot at again, too. I could hear the bullets hittin' the porch out there."

"How many shots did you fire?"

"I emptied my whole pistol. I don't keep a shell under the hammer, so that would make five shots."

"How many were fired at you?"

"Wasn't countin'. It sounded like a lot."

Rhodes took his teacup off the stove and pretended to drink. "Are you sure you've told me all you know about things out here, Mrs. McGee? You haven't left out anything at all?"

Ivy coughed, but Rhodes didn't look at her. He set his cup down and looked at Mrs. McGee.

The old woman stared back at him. "What makes you think I haven't?"

"It just seems that things keep happening around you. First we find a dead woman next door, then you shoot at one of your neighbors, now someone's taking a few shots at you. There's too much going on."

"We live in a terrible world," Mrs. McGee said. "It's not my fault that people are so rotten. I just do what I can and mind my own business."

"That's another thing," Rhodes said.

"What is?"

"That part about minding your own business. There are a few people around here who think you don't do that."

Ivy coughed again, louder.

Mrs. McGee put her own cup and saucer on top of the stove. There was quite a clattering as she did so. "Who says so? You tell me right now."

"I can't do that, Mrs. McGee," Rhodes said. "Is it the truth?"

"Of course not," she said. But she didn't look at him. Her watery eyes looked down at the fire burning in the stove.

"I think it is true," Rhodes said. "I think you know more than you're telling me, and I think someone wants to keep you from telling."

Mrs. McGee stood up with a speed that surprised Rhodes, knocking the rocker back several feet. "That's not so. You shouldn't say things like that to me. It's not so!"

Rhodes looked up at her. "I think it's so," he said.

"I'm not going to talk to you anymore," she said. "I want you to go now."

"I'll have to come back tomorrow," Rhodes said, standing up. "I have to check for evidence."

"You send somebody else. I don't want to talk to you."

Rhodes glanced at Ivy, who looked away. "I'll send Deputy Grady," he said. "Thank you for the tea."

* * *

141

"I can't believe you badgered an old woman that way," Ivy said when they were back in the car.

"I didn't badger her," Rhodes said. "She's been involved in a shooting scrape. I could have taken her in if I'd really wanted to badger her. I was being nice."

"Sometimes I don't think you're nice at all. You certainly don't know how to treat old ladies."

"That old lady's involved in a murder case."

Ivy was horrified. "She is not! Except that it looks like someone's trying to kill her."

"Where are we going?" Ivy said.

"To find out who made that phone call," Rhodes told her.

There was no light at Washburn's, but Rhodes got out and pounded on the door anyway. "Come on, Washburn. Open up," he called.

After a minute a light came on and Washburn came to the door. He was in a pair of blue pajamas, and his hair was tousled.

"What's going on, Sheriff?" he said.

"You know very well what's going on," Rhodes said. "You called my office not so long ago."

Washburn looked at first as if he were going to deny the accusation, but then he said, "All right. I called. So what? It sounded like a war zone around here. I thought that crazy old bat had started in on someone else, so I called."

"You're sure it wasn't you she started in on?"

"Of course I'm sure. What are you talking about?"

"I'm talking about you sneaking over there and taking a shot at Mrs. McGee."

"You must be crazy, Sheriff. Why would I do a thing like that?"

"That's what I'd like to know," Rhodes said, but he didn't find out, despite spending another thirty minutes talking to Washburn. He went back to the car knowing little more than he had before.

Ivy was silent most of the way back into town. When they were nearly to Rhodes's house, she said, "You don't think Mrs. McGee could have killed anyone, do you?"

142

Rhodes thought about it for a second. "She took a shot at Washburn. She took some more shots at someone tonight."

"I keep thinking of some of the things she said last night," Ivy said.

"What things?"

"She kept wondering if we were warm. She said we ought to keep wrapped up in this cold weather."

Rhodes wasn't sure he got the point.

"Don't you see? Wrapped up. That woman you found was wrapped up in the tape."

"That's a different kind of wrapping," Rhodes said, but he could see the point. Suppose Mrs. McGee had killed someone. Accidentally, of course. Seeing the body lying there, exposed, she might very well be seized with the desire to be sure that it was protected against the cold. Suppose that for some reason Mrs. Clayton had come over to Mrs. McGee's late at night, or even early. To borrow a cup of tea, or whatever. The old woman might have mistaken her for a burglar and shot her.

But how could you explain the fact that the body was nude under the tape? Mrs. McGee certainly wouldn't have stripped it.

All right, say Mrs. McGee was snooping around the Clayton house, saw something that frightened her, and cut loose with a volley of pistol fire. Say Mrs. Clayton was in the middle of some illicit act with someone. Washburn? Someone else? The someone else might have fled, leaving Mrs. McGee alone with the corpse.

It was possible, Rhodes decided, but there were plenty of other options. He still liked the idea that the burglars were caught in the act and committed murder to protect themselves, but suddenly he realized that there was a big flaw in that reasoning. He was going to have to settle himself down and think the whole thing through again.

"She might have done it," he finally told Ivy. "I'm just not sure. I'm not sure about anything in this mess."

Ivy patted his arm. "Don't worry. You'll figure it out."

He wished he could be as confident as she was.

Chapter 16

LAWTON WAS LEANING on a broom near the radio table when Rhodes walked into the jail the next morning. He and Hack had clearly been involved in a discussion. They turned at the sound of the opening door.

"Ella Click," Hack said.

Rhodes looked around to see if someone else was walking in behind him. "What?" he said.

"Ella Click," Hack repeated. "Works over in the county clerk's office."

It's too early in the day for this, Rhodes thought, but he said, "What about her?"

"She won," Lawton said.

"Good," Rhodes said. "Exactly what did she win?"

"The pool," Hack told him. "She had February twenty-eighth. Just missed it by one day. Unless you've changed your mind. You ain't changed your mind have you?"

"Haven't decided to put it off a while? Move it to a warmer month, like April?"

"No," Rhodes said.

"Well, I guess that's it, then. Ella Click is the winner."

"She's all right," Lawton said. "I know her mama. She used to be Ella Mitchum before she got married. Married Sam Click, and they got two kids. Sam works for the Highway Department. Started out wavin' one of those little flags like they do when they're workin' on the road, and moved on up to a pretty good job. But they can use the money."

"Sure they can," Hack said. "What would a couple of old reprobates like you and me do with all that money? Just spend it wastefully on big cigars and hard liquor."

"Maybe you're right," Lawton said. "But I could sure use me a new TV set. Old one of mine's got a line that runs right through the middle of the picture. Little black line, kinda wavy. Sometimes it runs right through the face of that guy who does the news on Channel Four."

"All right," Rhodes said. "I'm sorry you two didn't win the money. I didn't even know there was a pool. If anyone had told me about it, maybe I could have arranged for a date more in line with the ones you picked."

"Wouldn't have been no fun that way," Lawton said. "Besides, me and Hack ain't cheaters. We just wanted to win fair and square. Ain't that right, Hack?"

"That's right. 'Course if you was to have given us a little hint, like a friend might do, just some little hint about when you was plannin' to set the date, well, we mighta—"

"I said I was sorry," Rhodes told them. "Let's just forget it."

"I'll try," Lawton said. "But ever'time I see that little black line runnin' down that news fella's face . . ."

Rhodes decided his only course was to ignore them. He went over to his desk and looked down the list of U-Truck-'Em buyers again. There was no name on there that even resembled Melvin Holcomb, but he had some other options in mind.

Then the phone rang.

Hack answered, as usual. "Sheriff's office."

He listened for a few seconds. "Yeah, he's here. Just a minute." He put his hand over the receiver. "It's that Clayton fella."

Rhodes picked up the phone on his desk. There was only

145

one line into the jail, thought they did have two phones. Hack hung his up.

Clayton was plainly upset. "I want to know two things, Sheriff," he said. "I want to know if you've caught my wife's killer, and I want to know why you've been telling Washburn what I said to you about him. I thought that what I said to you would be kept in confidence."

"I'm still working on your wife's murder," Rhodes said. "One of the people I questioned was Washburn, and to get him to talk I had to tell him a few things. How did you happen to find out that I'd talked to him?"

"He called me, that's how!" There was a slight hiss on the phone line, and it made Clayton's voice sound more petulant than it probably was. "He wanted to know why I'd told you that he had a motive to kill Sula. That was just speculation, naturally. I didn't mean to imply that he was the killer."

"Of course not," Rhodes said. "He probably just misunderstood the way I told him about it. By the way, he told me that he did see your wife about the time she was killed."

"Ha!" Clayton said. "He did do it, didn't he?"

And this was the guy who didn't mean to imply anything, Rhodes thought. "He also told me that she was going to go back to Dallas and try to patch things up with you."

There was a brief pause, and Rhodes listened to the hissing of the wires.

"She didn't make it, did she?" Clayton said.

"No," Rhodes said. "I don't guess she did."

"She'll be buried today," Clayton said. "That's probably why I'm so upset. But I do want you to find her killer, Sheriff—soon."

"I'm doing my best," Rhodes said.

"See that you do." Clayton hung up without saying good-bye.

Rhodes looked at the phone thoughtfully, then went back to studying the list of van buyers. After a while he found what he was looking for, but he wasn't sure how much good it would do.

He spent the rest of the day writing reports and worrying

146

about the next commissioners' meeting, which was coming up in a week. He was going to have to tell them about the car wreck, but he thought that things would be all right. The car was still running, though it looked bad. He needed to take it to the repair shop so that the insurance adjuster could go by for a look at it when he was in town. Rhodes could use his pickup the next day when he went to the flea market.

Colton was a town that came alive only on the weekends, when its population doubled or tripled, and its streets were crowded with cars and pedestrians, most of them making their way to the flea market grounds on the edge of town. On the drive up, Rhodes had passed or been passed by ten or twelve pickups loaded down with items being carried to the sale. Old dressers, couches, bicycles, swing sets, desks, headboards for all kinds of beds, dogs, chickens, you name it. Rhodes thought the highway must have looked like it did in the thirties, when the dust bowl farmers were heading for California.

Rhodes himself didn't go directly to Colton. He stopped at the county seat for a visit with the local sheriff, Link Castle. They had met once or twice at statewide sheriffs' meetings. Rhodes wanted Link to call the Colton police chief and introduce him.

The county jail was quite a different sight from the one in Blacklin County. It was only two years old, and it had no windows on the outside. All the windows faced the exercise yard on the inside courtyard of the rectangular stone building.

The inside was even more different. There were four men and a woman in the office, all of them wearing gray uniforms. One of the men sat at a desk where he could watch several television monitors. One showed the exercise yard, the others the various cellblocks. Another of the men was doing paperwork at his desk. The woman was the dispatcher, and she sat at the controls of a much more modern radio than the one Hack used. It was the third man who caught Rhodes's eye. He was tapping away on a computer keyboard, and as

147

he tapped letters appeared on the small monitor in front of him. Hack would have loved it.

The fourth man was Link Castle, who looked like he was in training to be Rod Steiger's stand-in for a scene from *In the Heat of the Night*. He was a little older than Steiger, a little heavier, and a little balder, but the resemblance was there. He had a bluff heartiness about him that was all on the surface. The softness and heartiness hid the steely core of the man that Rhodes had heard speak about criminal investigation in a way that would have done the FBI school proud. He talked like a parody of a Texan, but anyone who took him for a fool would be sadly mistaken.

He shook Rhodes's hand and introduced him to the others. "This here's Sheriff Dan Rhodes," he said. "A famous lawman from down to the south a little ways. He's caught more killers in the last year or so than Sam Spade his own self."

The deputies turned from their work to say hello, then got busy again. Rhodes didn't think they were too impressed with him, which suited him just fine. He was always uncomfortable when people expected too much from him.

"Come on over here and have a seat," Castle said.

He led Rhodes to a big steel desk with a slick plastic top that was almost bare of papers. Rhodes envied the neatness of the place and wondered how Castle managed to keep his desk so clean. They sat in comfortable chairs that didn't squeak and were covered in what Rhodes assumed to be real leather. Obviously, Castle's county was not feeling the effects of the depressed Texas economy, or at least not very much.

"What can I do for you, Sheriff?" Castle said after settling himself into the chair and leaning back. "You didn't really say when you called."

"I'm looking for some people who burgled a few houses down in my area," Rhodes said. "I think they just might be up in Colton today, and I wanted to get the cooperation of the local law. I thought you might call the police chief up there and tell him I'd like to meet him."

"He'll be hanging around the flea market," Castle said. "If there's any crime in Colton, that's where it'll be from now to Monday."

148

"That's where I'm headed," Rhodes said. "I'd be glad to meet him there."

"I can call the office, have him paged. He could meet you there if you give him a time."

"How long does it take to drive?"

"You can make it in another fifteen minutes, easy. You might have trouble finding a place to park, but if you're in an official vehicle you can just drive right on the grounds."

"I'm in my own pickup," Rhodes said.

Castle looked at him suspiciously. "Don't make much sense to come on official business in your own private ride," he said.

Rhodes didn't want to explain about the wreck. "County car's out of service," he said.

"Oh. Well, in that case you'll just have to pay to park. Seems like half the people in Colton make a few bucks by chargin' the shoppers to park in their yards. But it ain't like it was Saturday. You ought to be able to park fairly close to the main gate. The office is right inside, little gray buildin' made out of cinderblocks. I'll call ahead and have Ed meet you. Ed Hamilton, that's the chief."

"Fine. I'd appreciate that," Rhodes said. They shook hands again and he left.

It took Rhodes a little longer than fifteen minutes to get to Colton because of the traffic. The weather had warmed still more, though a new cold front was expected in a day or two, and the sky was blue and sunny. People appeared eager to shop for bargains while the good weather held.

Rhodes parked in a vacant lot and paid three dollars for the privilege. He had to walk two blocks to the main gate, but on the way there he passed the overflow booths. There was no longer enough room on the official grounds for all the sellers, and they lined the streets all around the market. Down one street there were hundreds of animals for sale, dogs mainly, but Rhodes thought he saw a few cats, and there were a lot of rabbits and chickens. Men wandered through the crowd with rifles slung carelessly over their shoulders, the clips or breeches removed. They generally carried the rifles by the barrel, with the butts sticking up in the air.

149

Sometimes they would have a revolver or two or three stuck in their belts.

Rhodes went through the gate and saw the office immediately. It had a window on one side and a door in the front. The window was like the window of a fast-food restaurant. It slid open, and there was a broad ledge in front of it.

As Rhodes walked toward the office, he listened to the sounds around him. The whole area was filled with the voices of the buyers and sellers, the sounds of country and rock music coming from speakers all around, the barking of dogs, the crying of children. It was almost like the midway of a carnival.

Some of the rock music was blasting away in the office. Rhodes leaned in the window to talk to a short blond woman who was sitting at a small desk, reading a paperback copy of something called *Wild Night*. He felt the window ledge pressing into his stomach and remembered that he hadn't ridden the exercise bike in a long time, despite his promise to himself.

"I'm looking for Ed Hamilton," he said.

The woman put down her book. "Who?" she said, cupping her hand behind her ear.

"Hamilton, Ed Hamilton," Rhodes said as loud as he could without actually yelling.

"Oh, yeah. I paged him a while back. He ought to be coming along in a minute. You want me to try again?"

"If you don't mind," Rhodes said.

The woman didn't actually sigh, but she appeared to want to. She reached for a chrome microphone on a stand and pushed a button. "Will Ed Hamilton please report to the main office," she said. "Ed Hamilton, please report to the main office."

Her words, amplified a hundred times, came out of speakers located right above Rhodes's head. He resisted the urge to put his hands over his ears.

"He'll be along," the woman said. "Wears a black uniform. You can't miss him."

"Thanks," Rhodes said.

He turned to scan the crowd, and the woman got back to

150

reading her book. Rhodes watched the people milling around and tried to make out what was being sold at nearby tables. One of the main roads of the flea market ran down a steep hill, and in a few minutes Rhodes saw a man in black coming up it toward him. If Link Castle was Rod Steiger, Ed Hamilton was Warren Oates, leaning forward to climb the hill with just the right swagger and wearing just the right expression, an inch away from a sneer or a smile. He also wore his sidearm high on his waist. Rhodes waited until Hamilton had checked with the woman, then walked over and introduced himself.

"What can I do for you?" Hamilton said.

Rhodes explained who he was and why he was there.

"Penny didn't say anything about that," Hamilton said.

"I forgot to tell her who I was," Rhodes said. "I'm sure she got a call from Sheriff Castle, though."

Hamilton walked back over to the office and spoke to the woman through the window, then came back to Rhodes. "That damn Penny. She could've told me all that the first time. Now just what exactly is the problem, Sheriff Rhodes?"

Rhodes told him.

"Kinda shootin' in the dark, aren't you?"

Rhodes admitted that he was.

"Well, you might be able to find something out. Penny has a list of all the lots and who's rented them. If whoever you're lookin' for is actually here, and if they rented a lot and didn't just try to set up on the street somewhere, then she'll have a record of it. We try to discourage that settin' up on the streets, so I figure your main problem will be gettin' the information you want from Penny. Let me go talk to her."

Rhodes followed over to the window and listened to him give Penny detailed instructions.

"You got that?" he asked her.

"Of course I got it. You think I'm dumb?"

"Not the least bit," Hamilton said. He turned to Rhodes. "She'll give you what you need. I'd go with you to look, but I got to check in with the office about now. You have any

151

trouble, you just leave things alone and come after me. Penny can get in touch with me.''

It was clear to Rhodes that Hamilton thought he was on a fool's errand and wouldn't need any help for the simple reason that he wouldn't find what he was looking for. Rhodes thanked him anyway and watched him walk out the main gate. Then he turned back to Penny.

For the first time he noticed the computer keyboard and small monitor on the far side of the small desk. Her fingers were moving over the keyboard slowly as she tapped out the information she was seeking. Then she punched a key and words appeared in the middle of the screen.

''We don't have any Melvin Holcomb with a lot,'' she said. ''We don't have any Holcombs at all. We got a Harvey Holcombe, with an 'e,' on lot one-twenty-two, though.''

Rhodes got out a small notebook and wrote down the information. He would have to check it, but it didn't give him much hope.

''Now,'' Penny said. ''You want all the people whose initials are J.S.?''

''That's right,'' he said.

''Well, I can't get that very easily. I'll have to punch up all the last names starting with S and work from there. It's a lot of trouble.'' She looked wistfully at her book.

''I'd appreciate it,'' Rhodes said.

She moved her fingers over the keys, punched the command, and the names began to pop up on the screen.

There were five people who had the right initials, but no Jonathan Spence or Jeffery Sheldon among them. Rhodes hadn't thought it would be that easy. There was one very promising name, however. John Sheldon. Could be, Rhodes thought, but he wrote all the names and lot numbers down just in case.

John Sheldon was the one Rhodes would check first. Lot 247. Now all he had to do was find the right lot. He asked Penny how to get to 247.

She had already picked up her book again and started reading. Rhodes thought that he would have to remember the title and recommend it to Clyde Ballinger. This time Penny did sigh when she put the book down, but she opened the middle drawer of the desk and pulled out a photocopied map.

"All the lots are marked on there," she said as she handed it to him through the window. "Lot 247's way down in the flat. You go down the hill, turn left, and walk till you pass about five roads. You can count 'em on the map. Then turn right and go on down till you find 247."

Rhodes thanked her, but she had already picked up the book and started reading again. He looked at the map. The numbers of the lots were written in very tiny letters that he could hardly make out, and he found himself holding the map at nearly arm's length, trying to read them. It was the first time he had noticed himself doing anything like that, and he knew what it meant. He was going to have to get reading glasses. It was a depressing thought.

He finally located 247, approximately where Penny had said it would be, and started down the hill. He wondered if anyone would have reading glasses for sale.

Chapter 17

READING GLASSES were about the only things Rhodes didn't see. There were sunglasses galore, digital watches by the thousands, knives, dishes, tools, furniture, tricycles, bicycles, magazines, books, games, hubcaps, tires, video tapes (most of which Rhodes would bet were boot-legged), cassette tapes (ditto), pots and pans, barbed wire, beer cans, kerosene lamps, imitation-marble cutting boards, baseball cards, and a thousand other things.

It was easy to separate the professionals from the amateurs. The pros were there in bobtail trucks or in vans. They pulled into their lots, opened their doors, and set up sturdy wooden tables to display their wares. What they sold was mostly junk, but it was new junk. If it was old, it was in the collectible category, like the baseball cards.

The amateurs had come in their pickup trucks and lowered the tailgates to show off playpens and highchairs they no longer needed, old puzzles, back issues of "National Geographic," children's books with the covers missing, and food processors with cracked plastic bases.

There were more cars, trucks, vans, and pickups than Rhodes would have imagined.

And there were places to eat, too. Rhodes figured that the only people who could be sure of making a profit were the ones selling food, and since he hadn't eaten lunch, he decided to give one a try. He chose a huge wooden trailer that looked as if the owner had built it himself, out of plywood. Half of one side folded down to form the counter space, and Rhodes walked up and ordered a submarine sandwich with Hell on the Red sauce, and a canned Dr Pepper.

The sandwich tasted fresh, the sauce was hot, and the Dr Pepper was cold, so the meal met all Rhodes's requirements for fine dining. He finished, threw his napkin in the fifty-five gallon trash can, and went looking for lot 247.

He saw the green U-Truck-'Em van from a half block away, its roof showing up over the top of a canvas cover that extended from the camper top of a pickup parked next to the van. He walked down to the pickup and started looking at the goods displayed under the cover—an old black wash pot, some branding irons, a couple of lightning-rod balls, a rocking chair that had once had a wicker bottom and now had no bottom at all, and a wooden box that contained a socket set and a great many open-ended wrenches all jumbled together. Rhodes picked up one of the lightning-rod balls and pretended to study it while looking over the next lot.

A man about seventy years old, wearing a battered black cowboy hat, a tattered denim jacket, black pants, and worn boots got out of an aluminum lawn chair next to the pickup and walked over to Rhodes.

"You don't see many of them balls these days," he said in a raspy voice. "Look how milky that there glass is. You can tell there's been a charge through it. 'Course I won't charge you any more for that. If you're real interested, I got a couple of arrows there in the back of the truck. They still got the glass in them."

Rhodes said he was just looking and handed the ball to the old man, who took it and went back to his chair, clearly disappointed that he hadn't made a sale.

Rhodes strolled casually over to the next lot without look-

155

ing back at the old man. The back of the van was open, and he could see furniture and appliances stacked inside. On the ground were two refrigerators and several color TV sets, including a Sony and an RCA.

Between Rhodes and the van were several wooden tables. On top of the tables there were handmade wooden cases with glass tops and unfinished sides. Some of the jewelry was as familiar to Rhodes as the furniture and appliances; he had read descriptions of it and heard the Storms describe it. A man and a woman were sitting on beanbag chairs near the van. They were eating sandwiches, drinking canned Diet Sprite, and not paying too much attention to Rhodes until they saw that he was paying serious attention to the jewelry.

The man got up and walked over. "Need a ring for the little lady?" he said. He was slightly built but looked wiry and had a mop of thick red hair that needed cutting and combing. His eyes were a pale blue.

The woman looked at Rhodes curiously. She looked nothing like the man. Rhodes guessed her weight at around one-seventy-five, quite a bit of it fat, and he didn't think she would get off the chair for anything less than a catastrophic fire. She was chewing her sandwich slowly and with evident pleasure. Rhodes wondered why she was bothering with the diet soda, but then he realized that you saved your calories where you could.

"I'd like to look at that one there," Rhodes said, pointing through the glass to the diamond solitaire with the gold band, the one very much like the ring that Miss Storm had been wearing.

"Good choice," the man said. His voice was squeaky, as if it were still changing. "That's fourteen-carat gold, and that's a gen-u-wine diamond, not any of that cubic zirconium stuff."

The case was locked in the back with a small padlock through a hasp. The man got a key out of his pocket and was opening the lock when Rhodes heard someone call out, "Hey, Sheriff! Any luck?"

It was the police chief, Hamilton, walking along in front of the displays and waving.

"It's that goddamned law man," the woman yelled, but she was looking at Rhodes, not Hamilton. She began fighting her way out of the beanbag.

The red-haired man wasn't fighting anything. He was off and running in an instant, sliding between the van and the pickup as if he had been greased.

Rhodes jumped over the tables, or tried to. He hooked his left foot on one of the display cases and went crashing into the packed dirt on the other side of the tables. When he tried to get up, the woman hit him in the face with one of the chairs. Dust flew into the air and Rhodes flew back into the table, knocking them over and sending the display cases down, their glass shattering and the contents scattering.

"What the hell's goin' on?" Hamilton yelled.

The woman swung again, but Rhodes dodged the chair. "It's them," Rhodes said. "You take care of her." He dodged another swing, got to his feet, and ran between the van and the pickup after the wiry man.

He thought he heard Hamilton yell "Ummmmmmph!" as the bag hit him and the air went out of him, but he didn't look back.

The next road was crowded, but Rhodes could see the red hair bobbing along about half a block away, and he continued to run, thinking again how much good he would get out of a daily session on the Huffy.

The other man was clearly in better shape, but the crowd made running difficult, so Rhodes didn't lose any ground. He almost ran into a small boy, who took a swipe at him with his cotton candy, slowing him, but it didn't matter. The red-headed man stepped in a hole.

The roads through the flea market had been made by running a grader over the rough ground. They were tunneled from the rains and the grading had been none too smooth in the first place, far from ideal running surfaces. Rhodes was just glad he hadn't been the first to fall. By the time the man got to his feet, Rhodes had nearly caught up.

The man looked around him and found that he was in luck. He was right in front of a table of machetes, Bowies, and survival knives. He grabbed one of the machetes by its cheap

157

plastic handle and made several menacing passes in the air in front of him.

Rhodes was unarmed. He carried a pocketknife, but it was hardly a weapon and was useless in any kind of fight. It was mainly good to open letters with. He looked to his right and grabbed a bullwhip from among the leather goods on a table there. It was new and stiff, but when he lashed out it made a satisfactory popping.

The crowd had magically relocated itself. Now Rhodes and the red-haired man were almost alone in the road as everyone crowded into the booths nearby to see what would happen. They didn't know what was going on, but it looked more interesting than most things that happened at the flea market.

Rhodes, feeling only vaguely like Indiana Jones, swung the whip over his head and popped it again. His opponent didn't look the least bit impressed. He drew back his arm and threw the machete at Rhodes's midsection. Rhodes jumped aside and the knife clattered to the road behind him.

Then the little man was off and running again. He was wearing dirty leather tennis shoes, and he kicked up little puffs of dust as he ran. This time he didn't have a good lead, but he was gaining because the road had cleared in front of him. People all along the way pulled aside to see what was going on.

Rhodes still had the whip. He remembered that when he was a kid he had seen a lot of movies with Lash LaRue and Whip Wilson. Either one of them would have handled the fleeing man with ease, flicking the whip and tripping him up, but Rhodes didn't know that he was up to it.

He couldn't think of anything else, however, so he decided he'd better give it a try. He put on a burst of speed to get as close as he could, whirled the whip around his head, and lashed out for the man's feet.

The whip didn't pop, but to Rhodes's surprise it tangled up in the dirty Reeboks and sent the man tumbling forward. Rhodes was so surprised, in fact, that the fall jerked the whip out of his hand.

The man seemed less surprised by what had happened

than Rhodes, or maybe he was just adaptable. He continued to roll forward, gathering up the whip as he went. Then he rolled to the side, under a table, and stood up on the other side.

This table was covered with glassware, mostly tumblers that had once been given out as premiums to people who paid a little extra for their soft drinks at various fast-food restaurants. There were glasses with Tweetie Birds, glasses with Yosemite Sam, glasses with Bugs Bunny. Mr. Spock was there, along with Luke Skywalker, Han Solo, and the wookie. Rhodes didn't really have time to examine them because he saw most of them as they came flying at his head.

The redhead had a pretty good arm, and Rhodes couldn't avoid all the glasses. He did manage to take most of them on his arms and body, but he was afraid that he might be glassed to death if something didn't happen. Luckily, something did.

The owner of the glasses, seeing his wares shattering on the road, jumped on the redhead's back and bore him down. The redhead clobbered him in the side of the head with the likeness of Garfield, jumped up, and took off.

Rhodes found himself in hot pursuit again, or he assumed that it was hot pursuit. He was getting pretty warm, that was for sure, and he was also developing a stitch in his side. If this chase didn't end soon, he was going to collapse. He wondered why he couldn't chase people in his car, like they did on TV. The redhead had come to the bottom of the hill and started up.

Oh no, thought Rhodes, not the hill.

A dog dashed out from behind one of the tables and started biting at the man's ankles. That wouldn't have stopped him, but the dog ran between his legs, tripping him up.

Rhodes said a silent thank-you to the powers that be and charged forward. If he could stop him now, he wouldn't have to try running up the hill. But the slippery little man had other ideas. He got up again, kicked at the dog, and looked to see what weapons were at hand. What he found was much better for him and much worse for Rhodes. He was standing at a table of geodes, most of them between the size of an orange and a grapefruit. He began hurling them at the sheriff.

Again, Rhodes got his arms up, but the geodes were heavy and quite capable of giving him severe bruises if they didn't break his bones.

Rhodes dived under a table, then rose up, tumbling all the china thimbles that had been on it to the ground. Holding the table in front of him like a shield, he advanced on the rock thrower.

The geodes smashed into the table with solid thuds, taking big chunks of wood out of it each time they hit, but they weren't hurting Rhodes. When he got close enough, he tossed the table aside and confronted the man.

The man had his hand drawn back for a throw, leaving him open to almost any kind of punch. Rhodes slammed a left into his stomach and crossed over with a right to the chest. All the man's breath whooshed out and he fell flat on his tailbone, dropping the geode as he fell. He collapsed on the ground, and the little dog ran up and barked in his face.

As soon as he could catch his breath, Rhodes reached out and grabbed both the man's wrists, pulling him to his feet. Then he heard the sirens.

Too bad Ivy's not here, he thought.

The officers who arrived on the scene after having been called by Penny were named Cross and Buchanan. They drove Rhodes and the little man, whom they handcuffed, back to lot 247.

"Penny said there was a hell of a scuffle goin' on," Cross said. He was about twenty-five and looked eager to hear about the fight.

"There wasn't much to it," Rhodes told him. "This man may be guilty of a crime in my county and he didn't want to stay and talk to me." Rhodes had shown Cross and Buchanan his ID, but they still wanted to confirm things with Hamilton. "I think your chief might have a few charges to file against him, too, or at least against his friend."

"What friend is that?" Cross wanted to know.

"His lady friend. The last I saw of her, she was swatting the chief with a beanbag chair."

"Lord, he sure wouldn't like that. I wish—" Cross looked sideways at Buchanan and shut up, but Rhodes had the distinct impression that he was going to say, "I wish I could have seen that."

When they got to lot 247, the fight was over. The large woman was sitting back on her beanbag and Hamilton was standing in front of her with his pistol leveled at her head. He looked the worse for wear. His hair was mussed, his black uniform shirt was ripped, exposing a white undershirt, and the left leg of his pants was torn from the bottom to about the knee. He wore over-the-calf socks, Rhodes noted.

The woman also looked as if she had been through a battle. Her clothes were torn and she had a bruise on her left cheek. Like Cross, Rhodes found himself wishing that he had been there to witness what had happened.

"Glad to see you boys," Hamilton said when they got out of the car. "I got me a prisoner here that needs takin' in."

"Sheriff Rhodes has one too, in the car," Cross said "We got him cuffed."

"Well, cuff this one for sure," Hamilton said. "She's a damn wildcat when she gets started."

Buchanan, who still hadn't said a word, took out his cuffs and advanced on the woman.

"You touch me, I'm gonna kick you right in the family jewels," the woman said in a deep, Mercedes Mac-Cambridge voice.

Buchanan stopped.

"Don't mind her," Hamilton said. "I'd love a good excuse to blow her damn head off. She's already kicked me there."

Rhodes knew that he was going to have to revise his opinion of the woman. She was obviously not as lethargic as she had looked at first sight. Buchanan put the cuffs on her. She didn't kick him, but she twisted around and tried to keep him from getting hold of her wrists. When he did, she spat at him.

"I don't know for sure what you wanted with these two," Hamilton said to Rhodes, "but you can't have 'em for a while. I got 'em for assaultin' an officer, resistin' arrest, abusive language, and any other damn thing I can think of between now and the time we get 'em to jail."

"You can keep them," Rhodes said. "For a while at least. I'd just like to talk to them about a murder."

"I wouldn't be surprised if they did it," Hamilton said. "I wouldn't be surprised a damn bit."

Chapter 18

THE COLTON CITY JAIL was small and square, made of white brick. It had a flat roof, no windows, and sat on a lot right next to the City Library. In fact, the only difference in the two buildings was that the library had windows.

They took the prisoners in through the back door. Hamilton had agreed to allow Rhodes to question them after he got his own paperwork done, so Rhodes sat in the office while the couple was processed.

Their names were Joe and Anna Stephens, or at least that was what they had on their drivers' licenses. Rhodes wasn't too sure how accurate that might be. He thought it might be just another reflection of the group's affection for the J.S. initials. He wondered why it was that little things like that were so hard for people to change.

His hunch had been that somehow Burl and Lonnie were tied in with the Holcombs and maybe, by extension, with the burglars. In fact, he was now convinced that all six people were somehow connected in a scheme that involved theft, burglary, and probably a little dope deal on the side.

There was coffee in the office. Both Cross and Buchanan offered Rhodes cigarettes, but since he neither drank coffee nor smoked there was nothing for him to do but sit and wait. After almost an hour, Hamilton came in.

"You can talk to them now," the chief said. "We ran their names through the computer for both TCIC and NCIC, but they were clean. I hope you can get more out of 'em than we did."

Rhodes knew that TCIC and NCIC were the Texas and national computer networks. Though he didn't have a computer, Hack kept him up with the technology. He wasn't surprised that the names weren't in the networks. Considering the number of names this bunch had, he would have been shocked if they *had* been in there.

"I think I might be able to get them to say something," Rhodes said. "I have more to threaten them with."

The cell that held Joe Stephens was clean and warm. There were fresh blankets on the bunk, and the mattress looked firm. Rhodes was impressed. Joe was not. He was lying on the bunk, his wiry body relaxed, as if he didn't have a care in the world. He wasn't fooling Rhodes, however.

"Your wife's the driver, isn't she?" he said to begin the conversation. "She's the one who hit my car down there in Blacklin County."

Joe put his hands behind his head and gazed up at the ceiling. "I don't know what you're talkin' about."

"Sure you do," Rhodes said. "You may as well get it off your chest now. I can identify the truck. There'll be plenty of people who can identify the stolen goods. Melvin will be glad to talk to me if I let him off the burglary charges. You shouldn't have tried to sell the stuff so close to the scene."

Joe continued to stare upward. "I bought all that stuff," he said.

"And I'm sure you have a receipt," Rhodes said. "I'm not sure how that's going to help you with the murder charge, though."

Joe stiffened slightly, but he still didn't look at Rhodes. "Murder charge?"

Rhodes leaned against the cell door. The bars weren't

164

comfortable, but he wanted to appear as relaxed as the prisoner, if he could.

"That woman you killed during the burglary. That makes it capital murder, Joe. The death penalty."

Joe rolled over, put his legs over the side of the bunk, and sat up. He looked at Rhodes for the first time. "Nobody killed anybody."

"Wrapped her in duct tape, too," Rhodes said. "We've got your fingerprints on the tape."

That was a lie, of course, since as far as Rhodes knew the results of the tests hadn't been sent back from the lab yet. There hadn't been any prints found in any of the houses, for that matter, but Rhodes thought the lie was worth a try.

When Joe didn't say anything, Rhodes said. "That tape's sticky stuff, Joe. You should have known you'd leave prints all over it."

"We wear gloves," Joe said, his voice squeaking more than usual, as if he might be a little bit scared. "We always wear gloves."

"Somebody had to take off his gloves to tape the body," Rhodes said. "It's hard to peel that tape off the roll if you've got gloves on."

Joe looked around the cell, but he didn't see anything to help him, just the institutional-gray walls and the cell door. And Rhodes.

Joe shook his head. "All right. Let's say that those things we're selling came from some houses down in your county. It's possible that I might know something about that. But we didn't kill anybody. We might be thieves, but we're not killers."

Rhodes was almost certain the Joe was telling the truth. What had occurred to him earlier was that if Mrs. Clayton had been dead for three weeks, it would have been very unlikely for her to have been killed by the burglars. If they had been operating in the area for that long, someone would have reported them long before Mrs. McGee. The houses weren't used often in the winter, but someone would surely have paid a visit and noticed all his belongings missing within a three-week span.

Still, Rhodes thought that Joe might know something. He seemed nervous now, and he had laced the fingers of his hands together in his lap. Rhodes might not have all the latest scientific equipment available to him, but he liked to think that he knew how to read people. That was his strong point, and that was his focus in every investigation. Talk to people, try to read them, try to separate the lies from the truths.

"It won't work, Joe," Rhodes said. "We can place you in the house, we can place the victim in the house. You're good for it."

Joe tried to appear sincere. He looked right into Rhodes's eyes. "If I tell you something, will you go a little easy on us?"

"If you didn't kill her, then we can forget the murder charge," Rhodes said. "The other things, well, they'll have to stand.

Joe thought about it for a minute. "You got a cigarette?" he said.

Rhodes told him that he didn't smoke.

"Damn," Joe said.

"We can get you one from one of the officers after you say your say," Rhodes told him.

"We found the body," Joe said. "She was dead when we got there. It was pretty weird, finding her all wrapped up like that in the middle of the floor."

"She wasn't in the floor," Rhodes said. "She was in the closet."

"Yeah," Joe said. "Well, that's where we put her. We didn't feel like it was the right thing to do, you know? Walking all around her while we stripped the house. Somebody might've stepped on her. So we put her in the closet. Didn't figure it'd hurt anything. Like I say, we might be thieves, but we're sure not killers."

Rhodes believed him. "One other thing," he said. "Why did you crimp the ends of those icemaker outlets instead of just letting them run?"

Joe looked hurt. "Hey, I told you—we're thieves, man. We're not vandals."

Rhodes called Buchanan to see if he could get Joe a smoke.

166

After he got started, Joe was hard to shut up. He wanted to tell it all. Burl and Lonnie, it turned out, were his cousins. "They're just puttin' us up for a while in some old house they've got. Well, it may not even be their house, but there's no one in it right now, so we're usin' it. There's a shed out back beyond the barn where we can keep the truck. To tell the truth, it's not much of a place, but we didn't intend to stay long. Hell, we've only been here about a week."

The Holcombs were just friends. "We met 'em in California," Joe said. He was smoking his second or third cigarette. Buchanan had given him half a pack, along with a cup of coffee. "See, we've been doin' this for quite a while now, workin' our way across the country. We sell the stuff we steal and eat the canned goods we find. It's a pretty good living."

Rhodes didn't ask about the other burglaries. That would have to come later, and would probably clear up a lot of cases for a lot of local law-enforcement agencies when the word got out.

"Have the Holcombs been pulling that funeral home scam all along the way?" Rhodes asked.

"Yeah. Hell, nobody even noticed it till now, as far as I know. It was a real good deal. We could sell that jewelry for a lot less than you could buy it for at a wholesaler's even, and nobody likes to ask where you got it if they're buyin' it at a flea market. They probably know it's stolen."

He was probably right. Rhodes knew that most people found it hard to resist a bargain, even if they knew it wasn't strictly on the up and up.

"Did you notice anything else about that dead woman?" he asked.

"Nothin' to notice. There she was, wrapped up like one of those mummies in a museum. Didn't even know it was a woman till now."

"What about her clothes?"

"Mummies don't wear clothes." Joe flicked his ashes on the floor. "Least this one didn't."

"Were there any clothes in the house?"

167

"I don't remember one house from another, tell the truth. If there were clothes, we took 'em, though. We always do."

Rhodes supposed that he would have to go through all the items in the van, though he didn't think it would help. Hamilton had impounded everything, so it would be available.

"What do you think we'll be lookin' at for all this?" Joe asked.

Rhodes looked at him. "How many states did you go through?"

"I hadn't thought about that," Joe said. "Probably most of 'em won't even bother with us, though, will they?"

"Probably not," Rhodes said. "Not if you come clean on everything you did and help them clear the cases."

"Oh, I'll do that, all right," Joe said. "And Sheriff?"

"What?" Rhodes said.

"I really didn't want to get caught, but now that I am, I'm sorry I hit you with those rocks."

Rhodes rubbed a bruise that was forming just below his right elbow. "That's all right, Joe. I understand."

"I knew you would." Joe tossed his cigarette butt to the floor and stepped on it. "What kinda food you think they got in this place? Anna likes to eat, you know?"

"I guessed," Rhodes said. He called Buchanan to let him out.

It was late when he got back to Clearview, but Rhodes knew that Hack would be at the jail. Hack was always at the jail, even slept there. He had no family and practically gave his time to the county just to have a place to stay and something to do.

"Anything exciting happen?" Rhodes asked when he walked into the office.

Hack was sitting in his usual spot at the radio table. He didn't like to go to bed until around midnight. He said that he was too old to need much sleep.

"You first," Hack said. "You look like you had a little excitement."

"We got the burglars," Rhodes said. He told the story as

168

briefly as he could, leaving out most of the chasing and fighting.

"But they didn't kill that Clayton woman?" Hack said when Rhodes was finished.

"They say they didn't. I believe them. The timing's all wrong."

"At least you've cleared up the burglaries and the stealing at the funeral home. Clyde oughta be happy."

"We still don't have the jewelry back, though. It might be a while before Hamilton releases it."

"Long as you got it, ever'body'll be happy," Hack said.

"Maybe. Now, how about here?"

"Nothin' much. Ruth had to arrest Miz Reed Taggart. That's about all."

"All!" Rhodes said, falling into the trap. "Mrs. Taggart is the mayor's wife!"

"I know that," Hack said, hurt. "I keep up with the local politics."

"Why was she arrested?" Rhodes said.

"Shopliftin'."

"But the Taggarts have as much money as anybody in town," Rhodes said. "Maybe more." Taggart was a third-generation oil man, and the fact that oil was now worth only a fraction of what it had been a few years back didn't matter, not when you'd had oil in the family for that long.

"It wasn't because she didn't have the money," Hack said. "It was because she was ashamed."

Rhodes leaned back wearily in his chair. It had been a long day, and it looked as if it would be even longer. But eventually Hack would explain himself.

"Was she ashamed before or after she got caught?" Rhodes said.

"Both, I guess. But she was doin' it because she was ashamed."

"Doing what?"

"I told you that. Shopliftin'."

"Exactly what was she ashamed to shoplift?"

"It wasn't that she was ashamed to shoplift it, though I guess she was. She was ashamed to *buy* it."

169

"What?" Rhodes said. There was an edge to his voice.

"You don't have to get all huffy about it," Hack said.

"Tell me," Rhodes said, his tones clipped. "Now."

"Condoms," Hack said.

Rhodes wasn't sure he'd heard right. "Condoms?"

"That's what I said, ain't it?"

"Tell me the whole thing," Rhodes said. "From the top."

"The pharmacist at the drugstore caught her at it. She was puttin' 'em in her purse. Sheiks. You know about Sheiks?"

"I know. Get on with it."

"She wouldn't admit it, so Mr. Lee let her leave the store and called us. I sent Ruth, and she caught up with her and asked to see her purse. Poor woman broke down and confessed."

"Confessed what?"

"Confessed that she stole 'em."

"Hack, I swear . . ."

"No need for swearin'. I'll tell you. Seems she can't take those birth control pills anymore, and her husband thinks it's the woman's job to take care of things like that. But she was embarrassed to stand in the checkout line at the drugstore with a bunch of condoms in her hand. So she stole 'em."

"Ruth didn't really arrest her, did she." It wasn't a question.

"Well, no. But she could've. Mr. Lee didn't want to press any charges when he heard the story, and Miz Taggart paid him."

"I expect she was more embarrassed by all the goings on than she would have been if she'd just bought them in the first place," Rhodes said. What he was thinking was that he would have liked to have been there when Ruth Grady was telling all this to Hack. Hack would have been red as Joe Stephen's hair. "Anything else you need to tell me?"

"Ivy called, said to tell you to come by."

"I think I'll do that," Rhodes said. "That's the best offer I've had all day."

Chapter 19

THE NEXT MORNING Rhodes confronted Melvin Holcomb with the fact of Stephens's arrest. Melvin seemed surprised, but when Rhodes provided the details of their travels from California, Holcomb suddenly became willing to talk. He had pretty much the same story to tell as the one Rhodes had already heard from Stephens, though Holcomb was much more reticent about what had happened on their journey than Stephens had been. In fact, he refused to admit having taken anything from any funeral home other than the one in Clearview. He did admit that he had helped with the burglaries at the lake, and confirmed that they had found a body wrapped in duct tape in the middle of the floor and that they had put the body in the closet in the kitchen.

Rhodes also talked to Burl and Lonnie, who were saddened to hear of the capture of their cousin, though not surprised. They both denied having taken part in either the burglaries or the thefts at the funeral home, but they admitted that they had indeed provided shelter for their cousin and his friends.

"After all," Burl said, "he's kin, even if he is a criminal."

Both Burl and Lonnie appeared to believe possessing a little stash of dope was hardly a crime at all, certainly not in the league with burglary.

"We don't even sell it to anybody in the county," Burl said. "There ain't enough of a dope trade here to keep us in business. We generally take it up to Dallas if we want to sell it."

Ruth Grady questioned Mrs. Holcomb in her cell and got a story very similar to the one told by her husband. The thing that interested Rhodes was that neither one of them could explain their fascination with the initials J.S. In fact, neither one of them had noticed that their false names all began that way.

"It could be something they picked up from Stephens," Ruth said, and Rhodes thought that was as good an explanation as any.

"You realize this leaves us with fewer murder suspects than we had yesterday," Ruth said.

She and Rhodes were in the office with Hack, who was listening but who had no suggestions as to who might be guilty of murder. "I think you oughta be glad you solved two big crimes without worryin' too much about the third one," he said.

"The third one is the worst," Rhodes said. "It's the one we should really be worried about."

"Why? Whoever done it ain't killed nobody else."

"That we know of," Rhodes said. "Mrs. McGee's taken a few potshots around, and someone's taken a few at her."

"You don't think she did it, do you?" Ruth said. "She seems like such a nice old lady."

"Those are the kind you have to watch out for," Hack said.

"And then there are Clayton and Washburn," Rhodes said. "I think we ought to get Clayton back down here and talk to all three of them. There's something wrong in someone's story, and I have a feeling I should know it. Ruth, call that Officer Ferguson and have her locate Clayton for us. Tell her to get him down here this afternoon. If he doesn't want to come, see if she can bring him for us."

Ruth went to the phone.

Rhodes sat at his desk and began looking through the notes he'd made on his various conversations with the suspects. He had a feeling that everything he needed to know was in there, if he could just make sense out of it. After about an hour, he began to think that he had. It still didn't give him the whole story, but he was sure he had most of it.

Ruth Grady had already left on patrol, but she had gotten in touch with Dallas. Officer Ferguson was going to deliver Clayton to the Blacklin County jail, either alone or accompanied, by five-thirty that afternoon. Rhodes decided to make arrangements to have the other suspects there as well.

"Sounds like you been readin' Nero Wolfe books," Hack said.

Rhodes stared at him. "I didn't know you read mystery novels," he said.

"Don't anymore. I used to, a long time ago when my eyes were better and I could see that little print. I guess you don't look much like Nero Wolfe, though." Hack gave a significant glance at Rhodes's waistline. "Not yet, anyway."

Rhodes seemed to recall that Wolfe weighed in the neighborhood of a seventh of a ton. He thought again about the exercise bike that was gathering dust at his house.

"It might be interestin', though," Hack said. "Gettin' all the suspects together right here and all. I don't recall you ever doin' that before."

"We never had a situation exactly like this one before," Rhodes said. "Washburn's driving in on his own, but we'll have to pick up Mrs. McGee."

"You could have Washburn do that."

"I don't think so," Rhodes said.

"Why not?"

"We don't need to have two of the suspects riding together."

"You goin' to pull some trick that gets one of 'em to confess?" Hack said. "Nero Wolfe always had that police guy or that Goodwin fella ready to grab the guilty party."

"I'm not expecting a confession," Rhodes said. "If there is one, you can grab the culprit."

"I'm not grabbin' anybody. That ain't in my job description."

"Maybe Lawton would do it. I'll talk to him."

"Never mind," Hack said. "If you need any help, I'll take care of it."

"I thought you might."

Clayton was early, the first to arrive. He was smoking a Marlboro and seemed a little upset by the whole thing.

"I hope you got me down here to tell me you've caught the killer," he said.

Rhodes asked him to have a seat. "We haven't caught anyone," he said then, "But I think you could say we're narrowing down the possibilities. And you're going to get most, if not all, of your furniture and things back." He told Clayton about the burglary ring and about the van full of loot at the flea market.

Clayton looked around until Rhodes brought out the ashtray. "That's good news, I guess," Clayton said. "I was just about to file an insurance claim on that stuff."

"Well, you'd better wait a while. As soon as Hamilton releases it, you can claim what's yours, and I think we'll find a lot more in that house where they were living."

Just then, the door opened and Washburn walked in.

"What's *he* doing here?" Washburn said.

Clayton put his cigarette in the ashtray and stood up. "He's the one, isn't he?" Clayton said. "He's the one who killed my wife."

On the other side of the room, Hack was leaning out of his chair, ready to grab someone, when the door opened again.

Mrs. McGee, thoroughly garbed against the weather, walked in, followed by Ruth Grady. Rhodes thought he heard Washburn mutter the words "old snoop" under his breath. Ruth got Mrs. McGee a chair and asked if she wanted to take off her coat. She didn't.

"I don't know why you all keep it so cold in this place, but I suppose it is a jail, after all."

Rhodes felt uncomfortable after they were all seated. He

174

wished he had thought to ask Hack what Nero Wolfe said in similar situations. He had no idea how to begin, and he certainly wasn't going to say, "I suppose you're all wondering why I called you here."

Mrs. McGee came to his rescue. "Deputy Grady said you wanted to talk to me about that dead woman," she said.

"I want to talk to all three of you," Rhodes said. "I think I know who was responsible for everything now."

"About time," Clayton said, looking at Washburn. He got out another Marlboro and lit it.

"I wish you wouldn't smoke," Mrs. McGee said. "It's a terrible habit."

Clayton ignored her.

"I thought you might have killed her at one time, Mrs. McGee," Rhodes said.

The old woman looked at him resentfully from underneath the knit cap she always wore. "You ought to be ashamed of yourself, Sheriff."

"I probably should," Rhodes said, "but you were a little trigger-happy there for a while."

"And with good reason," she said. "Mr. Washburn came creeping up to my house, for one thing. And then someone shot at me."

"We need a section of your wall to get that bullet," Rhodes said. "It might be important evidence."

"I didn't shoot at myself, if that's what you think," she said.

"I'm sure you didn't," Rhodes said, looking at Washburn.

"Don't look at me," Washburn said. "I'm the one who called you to let you know it was happening. You don't think I'd do the shooting and then call it in, do you?"

"Ha," Clayton said.

Mrs. McGee looked at him and waved her hand in front of her face as if to clear away the smoke.

"That's what I thought for a while today," Rhodes said. "In fact, I thought that you had done it and then called up Clayton here to give yourself an alibi. You could blame the shooting on him, if you told him what I think you did."

"I told him that he was a lowdown rat for trying to pin things on me," Washburn said. "That's what I told him."

"You didn't happen to mention that Mrs. McGee was a snoop?"

Washburn glanced at the old woman. "Well, yes, I might have said that."

"Humph. I never heard such a thing," Mrs. McGee said.

"It's what he thought," Rhodes said. "I told you that, myself."

"You didn't say who," she said.

"No, I didn't. I thought he might have been trying to eliminate you because he thought you had seen too much. He said that you sneaked around and saw him and Mrs. Clayton once."

"I didn't sneak." Mrs. McGee was disdainful. "I was just walking around and heard something. So I had me a look. That's all there was to it."

"And what did you see?" Rhodes asked.

"They were just arguing. I've seen worse."

"You walk around a lot, then?"

"Some. I can't sit on the porch all the time."

"That might worry someone who didn't know exactly what you might have seen," Rhodes said.

"Then it didn't worry me," Washburn said. "I knew exactly what she'd seen, all right."

"Of course it would be easy for me to check that phone call with the local office," Rhodes said. "I could check to see when it was made, whether it came before or after the shooting."

Washburn thought about it. "It was before, I'm pretty sure."

"So what," Clayton said. "He could have called before and then gone to do the shooting."

"It would have been smarter that way," Rhodes said. He turned to Mrs. McGee. "What does Mr. Washburn look like to you?"

"What do you mean?" she said.

"I mean, what kind of person."

"Oh. Well, he looks like a hippie, with that beard."

176

Rhodes wondered how long it had been since he'd heard anyone called a hippie. "He doesn't look like an insurance salesman? A greasy and slimy one?"

"Well of course not. He could do with a shave, though, I'll say that for him. Otherwise, he seems very clean."

"Now why do you think anyone would call him greasy?" Rhodes said.

"I have no idea."

"Me either," Rhodes said, "unless it was an attempt to prejudice me."

Clayton blew smoke. "Hey," he said. "So I don't think he looks good. So what?"

"Nothing," Rhodes said. "Unless I think that you came down here and tried to kill Mrs. McGee after that phone call. Not knowing what an old snoop might have seen, you decided to get her out of the way."

"You're crazy," Clayton said. He butted the cigarette in the ashtray.

"Maybe. Or maybe you still have the pistol. You didn't get rid of it after you shot your wife with it, did you? A bad move if you didn't."

"I don't have any pistol. Come on. You're making all this up."

"There's another thing," Rhodes said. "The first time you were in this office, you told me that you'd been to your house at the lake, searching for your wife. Isn't that right?"

"I guess so. I don't remember."

"I do. And you said—before you accused Washburn—that maybe the burglars had killed her."

Clayton appeared relaxed. "So?"

"If the burglars had been there before the murder, which they hadn't, don't you think you might have noticed that everything in the house was missing? I know you were looking for your wife, but still, a thing like that . . ."

Clayton leaned forward in his chair, his fists clenched on his knees. "That's thin, Sheriff. Really thin. Why would I just leave my wife dead in the house?"

"It's better than having her dead at your house in Dallas, which is where you probably shot her. I suspect you were tired of her affair with Washburn, even if she did try to patch things up."

"That's right," Washburn said. "She told me that she was going back to talk to him. He didn't listen. That's when he did it."

"You're full of it," Clayton said.

"I don't think so," Rhodes said. "I think you killed her there, wrapped her in the tape, maybe to confuse things like the time of death or maybe in the hope that she wouldn't putrefy too soon. You brought her back in her own car, the Ford Escort, then drove it back to Dallas yourself. I imagine you parked it in a convenient spot and left the keys in it, so no telling where it is now. I suppose you hoped that the body would be found and that Washburn would get the blame. Or if not Washburn, anyone except you."

Clayton leaned back and laughed. It wasn't much of a laugh, but it was still a laugh. "You sure do use the words 'think' and 'imagine' a lot, Sheriff. If you could prove a word of that, I might be worried."

"You're right," Rhodes said. "That's what I believe is the truth, but you don't have to worry about it."

"Right," Clayton said.

"What you have to worry about is the fingerprints."

Clayton sat forward. "Fingerprints?"

"On the duct tape," Rhodes said. "All over it."

Clayton came out of his chair like a shot, pushing Rhodes aside, bowling over Mrs. McGee, and stiff-arming Washburn as he made for the door.

As quick as he was, Ruth Grady was quicker. She didn't bother to pull her sidearm. There were too many civilians around. As Clayton reached for the doorknob, she grabbed him by the collar and jerked backward. Clayton made a gagging sound, and his head snapped back. As he stood there choking, Ruth spun him around and sank a hard right into his stomach. Clayton sat on the floor, hard, making sounds like a gut-shot mule.

Washburn was on his feet again. "I knew he did it, the son of a bitch."

"Watch your language," Hack said. He was helping Mrs.

McGee off the floor and back into her chair. "There are ladies present."

Rhodes recovered himself and walked over to where Ruth stood by Clayton. She had her pistol out and pointed at his head.

"I think he's harmless now," Rhodes said.

Clayton had his hands at his throat and was alternately gagging and trying to suck in a breath. There was no likely way he could get up and cause anyone any harm.

"I woulda got him," Hack said. "But I wasn't close enough. Nero Wolfe always has that Goodwin fella right by the chair where the murderer is sittin'."

"You did fine," Rhodes told him. "You, too, Ruth. Thanks."

"I declare," Mrs. McGee said. "This has certainly been an unusual experience. It's better than anything I ever saw on television."

"It's not quite this lively all the time," Hack said.

She looked at him closely. "Aren't you Hack Jensen?"

"Yes'm, that's me."

"You used to be friends with Fibber," she said.

"That's right, sure enough," Hack said.

"Are you married?"

"Uh, no ma'm."

"Well, you might still come for a visit. You're a fine-looking man."

"Uh, well, we're usually pretty busy here at the jail," Hack said weakly. Rhodes thought he might be blushing.

"I'm sure the sheriff would give you some time off. Wouldn't you, Sheriff?"

"I think it could be arranged," Rhodes said.

Hack glared at him.

"I might even start a pool," Rhodes said.

"What's that, Sheriff?" Mrs. McGee said.

"Oh, nothing," Rhodes told her, looking at Hack. "Just a private joke."

"Speakin' of private jokes," Hack said when everyone was gone and things had calmed down considerably. "When

179

do you reckon we'll get the results of the fingerprint tests back from that lab?''

"I don't know," Rhodes said. He smiled. "It might be another week or two. They always are a little slow.''

"Think there's gonna be evidence of any prints when it does come back?''

"You never can tell," Rhodes said.

Chapter 20

RHODES FIXED CHILI that night and thought that it turned out very well, considering the fact that Ivy wouldn't let him put the beans in it.

"You're not supposed to put beans in chili," she told him. "You can have beans on the side if you want to, but you never put them in the pot while the chili's cooking."

"Next you're going to tell me that I can't put ketchup in it," he said.

"You can do that, but not while it's cooking. Afterward, when you're eating it, it's all right. At least it is with me. Some people wouldn't agree."

"How about the crackers?"

"Everyone eats crackers with chili. It's practically required."

"That's not what I mean. I mean, can I crumble the crackers up and drop them in the bowl?"

"It seems sort of messy, but I understand that's what all the most knowledgeable chili eaters do."

"Good," Rhodes said. "That's the way I like to do it. You're sure about the beans?"

"I'm sure."

As it turned out, Rhodes liked the chili without the beans, though he managed to slip a few spoonfuls into his own bowl when Ivy wasn't looking. "It's supposed to be made with chili meat," he said, "but I like it just fine made with this ground chuck, don't you?"

Ivy agreed that she did, even if the texture wasn't quite right.

"Who's going to do the cooking after February twenty-seventh?" Rhodes asked.

"We'll see. Maybe we can take turns. Did you put any jalapeños in this?"

"A few," Rhodes said. Actually, he couldn't say for sure how many of the peppers he'd put in. He'd had only nacho slices, so he just dumped in whatever was in the jar. "Is it too hot?"

"Just right. Could you get me another glass of water?"

Rhodes put more ice in the glass and filled it with water.

"Thank you," Ivy said when he handed the glass to her. She drank half of it at one swallow, then put the glass on the table. "Are you glad the murder case is solved?"

"It's solved, but it's not over," Rhodes said. The chili seemed just right to him, too. "We'll get an indictment, but after that, things get shaky."

"Don't you have a good case against Clayton?"

"Only if the lab actually finds fingerprints on that tape. Otherwise, it's all speculation."

"It's hard to convict on speculation." Ivy took another bite of chili and another long drink of water.

"We have one other good chance of pinning it on him. The Dallas police will be getting a warrant to search his house. I'm willing to bet that they'll find the murder weapon, and that it'll also be the gun that fired the shots at Mrs. McGee. Ruth brought in that section of wall and we got the slug out of it. I'm sure the ballistics tests will show it was fired from the murder weapon."

"Do you think Hack likes Mrs. McGee?"

Rhodes put down his spoon and grinned. "I think she likes

him. I'm not sure that old guy will ever take the hint and go for a visit.''

"What about all those other people in the jail?"

"We do have a crowd," Rhodes said. "It would be even worse if Hamilton would let us have the Stephenses. Anyway, they'll all make bond before long and then we'll have to try to keep track of them. Burl and Lonnie don't have much to lose. It's a first offense, so they'll probably stick around. The others, well, they're used to living off the fat of the land and they might try to get tricky."

"What about all those other burglaries that Stephens admitted?"

"We'll be getting some inquiries, you can count on that. But it's like I told Joe. If Stephens is convicted here, the other states won't bother with him as long as he'll tell what he did and let them clear the books. It's not as if he's dangerous. He's proud that all he does is steal."

"Then things ought to calm down for a while."

"They should. Why?"

"I was just thinking." Ivy put down her spoon and looked at Rhodes. "February twenty-seventh seems like such a long way off."

All at once the inside of Rhodes's mouth felt hot and dry. Sure enough, he had put too many jalapeños in the chili. He took a deep drink of water, so fast that he almost choked.

"Excuse me," he said. He got up from the table and walked over to the sink, turned on the tap, filled his glass, then drank it down.

"Your face looks red," Ivy said.

"Chili got too hot all of a sudden," he said.

"You're sure it was just the chili?"

"Sure I'm sure. What else could it be?"

"That's what I was wondering."

"Well, that's what it was. Do you hear the dog scratching at the back door? He probably thinks I'm not going to feed him tonight."

They walked together to the door. Rhodes opened it, but Speedo was not there. Rhodes whistled. The dog poked his head out of his barrel and looked at them.

183

"Come on, boy," Rhodes said. "Time for supper." He got the dry dog food and poured it in Speedo's bowl.

They watched him eat. "His real name is Mr. Earl," Rhodes said. "It's from a song."

"I think I remember that one," Ivy said. "Do you think he'd like living at my house?"

"Your house?"

"We have to decide about that, whether we're going to live in your house or my house."

"That's right," Rhodes said. "We have to decide that."

The telephone rang inside the house.

"Got to answer that," Rhodes said.

He put the dog food up and they went back into the house. Rhodes got to the phone on about the fourth ring. He listened for a long time.

"What's the trouble?" Ivy said when he hung up.

"Some man at the Jolly Tamale. He's locked himself in the women's restroom and won't come out."

"The women's restroom?"

"The one that says 'Señoritas' on the door."

"I know that. But why?"

"He says that it's an example of sex discrimination. That restroom is always cleaner than the men's room. He's not coming out until the management says they'll keep them both the same."

"What was he doing in there in the first place?"

"They don't know that yet."

"And you're the one who has to find out?"

"It looks that way. You want to come?"

"Siren?"

Rhodes thought about it. "Why not?" he said.

"Let's go," Ivy told him.

184

About the Author

Bill Crider's first Dan Rhodes mystery, *Too Late to Die*, received the coveted Anthony Award for Best First Mystery Novel. *Death on the Move* is the fourth in the series, that also includes *Shotgun Saturday Night* and *Cursed to Death*. Crider has also written a number of critical works and short stories. He lives in Alvin, Texas, with his wife and their two children, and is chairman of the English Department at the community college there.